Jwa
5/21/82

"GO INSIDE THE CORN ROWS,"
SHE WHISPERED.

After a moment there was a rustling of corn stalks; she had followed him. She stood up over him, then she reached down and caught the shapeless dress below her knees and slowly pulled it upward.

Longarm caught his breath. She wore no underthings. She slipped the old dress over her head, taking her straw hat along with the garment. The flaxen hair spilled back across her naked shoulders. He had never seen such fresh young loveliness.

He took her breast in his hand. With part of his mind, he wondered how he was going to accomplish very much with his legs chained and shackled. But he was sure as hell going to find out....

D0824323

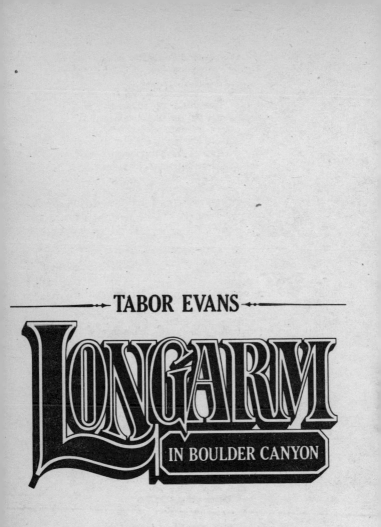

TABOR EVANS

LONGARM

IN BOULDER CANYON

A JOVE BOOK

LONGARM IN BOULDER CANYON

A Jove book / published by arrangement with
the author

PRINTING HISTORY
Jove edition / May 1982

All rights reserved.
Copyright © 1982 by Jove Publications, Inc.
This book may not be reproduced in whole or in part,
by mimeograph or any other means, without permission.
For information address: Jove Publications, Inc.,
200 Madison Avenue, New York, New York 10016.

ISBN: 0-515-05600-6

Jove books are published by Jove Publications, Inc.,
200 Madison Avenue, New York, N.Y. 10016.
The words "A JOVE BOOK" and the "J"
with sunburst are trademarks belonging to
Jove Publications, Inc.

PRINTED IN THE UNITED STATES OF AMERICA

Chapter 1

Stepping off the westbound Union Pacific limited and onto a half-lit, unroofed station platform, Longarm caught his breath and swore aloud.

Slanting rain struck him in the face with the force of a hundred punishing fists. The relentless pummeling and the insanity of rain in the desert set off alarm bells inside his skull. Everything in the world was suddenly gone crazy, turned upside down.

"Goddamn," he said aloud. "Rain's the plumb last frigging thing I need right now."

Rain.

Rain was bad enough, even where it could be expected. Rain in the desert was unspeakably worse. Rain striking in the desert is as unreal as it is unlikely. When it does let go, Lord help the man caught in it. The bottom falls out of the sky. Desert rains are gully-washing thunderstorms or they're nothing. And the hell of it is, the greatest single danger a man faces on a desert—including hunger, thirst, sidewinders, and heat prostration—is drowning. And that's because huge, eternal stretches of desert can be long-dry bottoms of what would be

1

lakes or rivers in more sensible regions, and may even once have been vast estuaries in more reasonable times. A man learns—or fails to live to regret—that on those rare occasions when it does rain in the desert, he can find himself swimming for his life in the torrent of what had looked like arid wastes.

And a rainstorm in the black of the night in a strange settlement in the middle of nowhere—that added insult to misery. Volleys of lightning erupted, blasting the skies and the distant gray hills a dazzling white, and teeth-shaking thunder discharged, exploded, echoed, and then flared again in the recoil of its own mindless violence.

Rain pelted the dry, sere earth and ran off as if the sand were oiled. Even when puddles formed, the drops still beaded, as if the ground lay polished with water repellants.

Longarm didn't consciously think any of this as he sprinted from the car exit toward the six-inch overhang at the lighted window of the depot waiting room; these half-formed ideas just wheeled and raged through his brain between cusswords.

Behind him, in the warmth, comfort, and security of the coach entry, the conductor laughed, waved, and yelled his taunting farewell. "Good luck, Marshal! Keep your pecker dry."

"Go to hell, you potbellied bastard." Longarm turned, squinting against the rain. He bit down hard on his sodden, limp, and drooping cheroot. He was a big man, lean and muscular, kept hard and fit by trying to stay alive in places just as ornery as this.

Under the rain-dripping brim of his snuff-brown Stetson, positioned carefully on his close-cropped head, dead center, there was nothing young about his face. It was seamed and sun-cured to a saddle-leather brown. There was no sign of softness in him, certainly in the gunmetal blue of his narrowed eyes, which glinted in the faint window light. His hair, brows, and neatly waxed longhorn mustache were the color of aged tobacco leaf.

In less than a minute his frock coat, gray flannel shirt, woolen vest, and skintight brown tweed pants were rain-soaked and clinging to his hide. He struck hard against the waiting-room door and bounced off because it was locked.

From the lighted train the conductor laughed loudly. "Ain't you got sense enough to git in out of the rain, lawdog?"

2

Longarm didn't even bother turning around. With the rain whipping at him mercilessly, he stood in a wan rectangle of light and pounded on the door.

Behind him, the belly-laughing conductor reached out his arm far enough to swing his lantern in a circular motion, signaling the engineer to head out.

As the engine hissed, gathering speed, Longarm felt his heart sink for no explainable reason.

When the westbound limited got up a head of steam and coughed its way west through the ravening thunder squall, the town and the valley were engulfed abruptly in a blackness that fit so snugly it felt almost suffocating. The stygian darkness settled in with the rain, chopping off the known cosmos at the saffron rim of lantern light glowing at the brink of the freight platform.

Longarm knew there was a town beyond that faint fingering of light, but he could not see its sun-bleached gathering of buildings, houses, and barns. His ticket had named Carp, Nevada as his destination, and here he'd been ushered out into the black, wet night. The only commerce in Carp was mining, as far as he knew. There was no other reason for its existence except the poverty-level placer mines staked out in the region. In the seventies, a mill had been erected near the river, and the ore from the diggings came in on mule-drawn carts. Once, the diggings had turned up yellow treasure and the mines and the mill paid well. By now strikes were few and the labor tough and unrewarding. There were not many deposits anymore that could be worked with pick and shovel; a placer miner needed the investment of hydraulic pressure to dislodge the pregnant gravel into the sluice boxes.

In the darkness and thunderstorm the town was quiet, turned in on itself like a terrified armadillo.

Longarm could see the stationmaster moving around inside the lighted waiting room, but the man paid no attention to his beating on that locked door.

Abruptly the light inside the building was doused. The faint lantern light on its peg glittered wanly in the gray sheeting of rain.

Wearing a rain hat and oilcloth slicker, the stationmaster emerged from the freight doors. He locked them with a large brass key, which he dropped into his coat pocket, quickly closing his slicker over his clothing. He wore knee-length, wet-weather boots and clomped along the platform with his head down. He did not bother to look up when Longarm yelled at him.

The station manager reached the single lantern. Longarm yelled, "You son of a bitch, I'm talking to you! Are you deaf or just ornery?"

The depot master turned down the wick on the platform lantern before he answered. "What's eatin' you, mister?"

"You are, you peckerhead. I just came in on that train—"

"Saw you. You're here. You rode our train. We don't owe you nothin' more."

"Jesus Christ. It's storming. Or haven't you noticed? Can't you even tell me where I can get a room?"

The man kept his hand on the lantern key. He shrugged, rain dripping from his flop-brimmed rain bonnet. "Might find a room up over the saloon. Humble Earl's saloon."

Longarm glanced around helplessly. "That might as well be in hell in this darkness. Where is Humble Earl's saloon?"

"Yonder." The man gestured vaguely into the darkness. He considered a moment and then laughed in a flat, unfriendly way. "May need a rowboat to get there from here."

"Never mind that. Just point me in the right direction."

The stationmaster hesitated a moment, then pointed out into the rainswept blackness. "See that faint yellow glow? That there's Humble Earl's. Can't miss it. Only place in town that's still open at this hour. Yep, them yeller beacons are your lighthouse though if you ask me—and you didn't—you'll be safer here till the next train goes through at dawn."

"Now why in hell would you say a thing like that? You don't know me, do you?"

The man shrugged again. "Don't have to know you, mister. I know why you're here. That's all I have to know."

"What makes you think you know why I'm here?"

"Mostly only ones ever git off the limited are just like you. After one thing."

"Yeah?"

"You're here looking for Little Billy Bates, ain't you?"

Longarm chewed on his sodden cheroot, which hung down along his chin now.

"And what if I am?"

The man shrugged those spindly shoulders again. "Just take my word for it. You're safer out here in the rain till you can

4

git on the eastbound—if you can make it."

"What makes you think I won't make it?"

The rain-dripping head tilted, the sun-bleached eyes glittered in lanternlight. "Hell, mister. Was I a bettin' man—which I ain't—I'd give you odds you don't make that train out of here—or no other'n, neither."

"What makes you so goddamn optimistic?"

"You're a stranger in Carp, ain't you?"

"That's right."

"And you're lookin' to take Master Bates in—right?" When Longarm didn't answer, the depot manager laughed gratingly in the wetness. "Hell, mister, I figure do I see you again, 'twill be in a pine box marked for shipment back where you come from."

Raging inwardly, Longarm exhaled heavily and spat the dank cheroot to the platform and watched the man turn down the lantern wick and blow it out.

They were plunged into breathless darkness. The afterimage of the lantern danced crazily behind Longarm's eyes. He closed his lids tightly for a few seconds, hoping to acclimate himself to the blackness, to be able to make out at least dim outlines. But when he opened his eyes again, he saw only vague, purple-ringed refractions of the lantern light.

In the darkness, the stationmaster said, "Well, good night, stranger."

Before Longarm could speak to delay him, the rail-thin man stepped off the end of the platform and was gone. There was the receding splash of his boots in the deepening rivulet of the street, and then no sound at all except the pounding of rain, the reverberation of thunder.

A sizzling eruption of lightning illuminated the rain-hammered main street with its houses, stables, stores, and saloon.

In the frenzy of thunder, Longarm stepped off the platform in calf-deep, swift-rushing water, and plodded toward his memory of the briefly lit saloon.

The savage rain raged in its fury, battering the town, blanketing all other sound. The going grew tougher as he waded toward a dim but brightening yellow glow. The water rose swiftly in the street and the temperature had fallen perhaps ten degrees since the storm hit. He glanced back toward the blob of the depot, and then at the distant lights.

He hesitated, his jaw taut. The rising water sogged his tweed trouser legs and lapped at his boots. It was slow going in the rising water. Unseen things bumped his calves and then swept past on the raging current.

After every new and breathtaking blast of lightning, the world darkened into deeper, more cavelike blackness. The faint glow of barroom windows seemed to recede in the night.

He stepped into a deep wagon rut. Twisting his ankle, he stumbled and nearly fell. He managed to catch his balance and hang on to his carpetbag. His breath quickened and he recognized the growing danger of his journey as he angled across the wide main street that was suddenly a fermenting tributary of the Colorado River.

He felt as if he could hear the tumultuous roaring of that full-bellied stream. Carp was thrown together on its banks. The limited had inched across a steel trestle just before it halted at the depot long enough to spit him out into the wet blackness.

He plodded forward, feeling his way. Another rut or pothole could throw him. He was already wet enough, mad enough, disgusted enough. He didn't need to fall and be hurled along on this growing torrent of water.

He sloshed, crabbing his way, stepping carefully as a blind man might, keeping the gleam in those barroom windows ahead like the hope of heaven. And yet, as the station manager had warned him, no haven of safety awaited him in Humble Earl's Saloon. And why not?

Teeth clenched, he answered his own question. Because he was guilty of the single most unpardonable sin in these parts: he was a stranger in town. Inside him a reckless obstinacy built, as if his blood boiled with liquor.

He quickened his steps, because what he needed right now was to get into something dry—like straight Maryland rye.

The long glitter of lamp glow reached out to him in the darkness. Sighing, he stepped into the rim of light. He felt cautiously with his boot for a boardwalk. He'd almost made it.

From behind him, as he entered the weak rectangle of light, a gun fired twice. Bullets splashed into the water beside Longarm like lethal wasps.

Moving almost involuntarily, Longarm grabbed his double-action Colt Model T .44-40 from its cross-draw rig.

In that same motion he wheeled around and stepped out of the light, firing three times in rapid succession toward the unlighted building behind him, from which the gunfire had

6

come. It was difficult moving in the swift, rising water, but rage and self-preservation prodded him.

Across the street, a man yelled in terror. In a flare of lightning, Longarm saw a tall, lean man running along a veranda. The bushwhacker, whoever he was, had lost interest in an ambush where the target shot back.

His heart thudding crazily, and blood pounding in his temples louder than the rush of the swollen river, Longarm holstered his gun and sprinted up onto the sheltered veranda of Humble Earl's.

Panting, Longarm pressed his back against the rough-textured wall. Shivering slightly, he shook himself dry and gandered around the black night-town.

Goddamn, he thought, what a hellhole. It grew crazier by the minute. A rainstorm in the desert. A man who smilingly bets you that you won't live till morning. And now a backshooter who didn't even bother to introduce himself, or to explain his hate.

Welcome to Carp, Longarm...

Humble Earl's saloon was a high-ceilinged place, sporting rooms around an open second-floor balcony. Even the newel posts, railings, and banisters were hand carved and fancy. The windows were closed and the folding doors had been set over the batwings to keep out the rain and chill. It was easy to believe this was the best-constructed edifice in town, glowing with lights that danced on polished bar and tabletops. Outside, the storm raged and the night was miserable and silent.

Inside Humble Earl's there was laughter and boisterous talk; the place pulsed with noise and excitement. Here was the heart of Carp—if such a settlement could be said to have that organ. Hazy clouds of blue smoke drifted between the stained-glass lampshades, reaching upward to the busy balconies. Men in derbies, Stetsons, and shapeless felt hats draped themselves the length of the bar or crouched over cards and hooch at tables. They shouted over the pounding of rain against the walls, talking of the storm or arguing over the few women or the fall of poker hands.

Longarm closed the folding doors behind him and set his bag down against the wall.

The shouting ceased, the laughter muted, and the voices abruptly lowered. Men and women at bar and tables stopped talking and stared at Longarm as he slapped water from his coat and hat.

These people watched him curiously and coldly, taking in the heft of his six-foot-plus body, the width of his shoulders, the musculature of his legs and thighs in pants that adhered wetly to his skin. It was clear in their faces: he was not welcome here. He was a stranger. They didn't know him. They didn't like him without bothering to know him. They didn't want to know him. They didn't want him in their town.

Longarm shook off some of the rain, staring back at them. The hell with them. He walked across the sawdust-sprinkled flooring, his boots making a squishing noise. Water ran down his face and into his eyes.

It was some moments before Longarm could get accustomed to the warmth and garish light in the saloon. He found an empty place at the bar. The two men nearest him moved away, gazing at him as if he were a bill collector or a leper.

The bartender leaned across the bar, smiling at him flatly. His mustached lip twisted into the semblance of a smile, but the warmth never reached his puffy brown eyes. Obviously the bartender shared the town's antipathy toward him, but after all, business was business, and a stranger's money was as good as anybody else's, as long as he lived to spend it.

"Howdy, mister." The bartender wore his thinning black hair parted, slicked down in a wave over his high forehead. His white shirt was stained at the armpits and streaked with beer, as were his vest and apron. It looked as if he ran the only gold mine in the area that was really paying off anymore. "I'm Earl Willis." He laughed stridently. "People call me Humble Earl because humble is the main thing I ain't. I own this here establishment."

Longarm nodded. "Name's Custis Long."

"Come far?"

Longarm glanced around at the watchful men, the unsmiling women. "Maybe too far."

Humble Earl didn't pretend to misunderstand. "Could be," he said, his eyes narrowing slightly. "Was that gunfire we heard just before you come in?"

"Reckon. I heard it too."

Earl Willis nodded. There was no surprise in his fat face as he said, "We thought maybe it was thunder. But it was too sharp-like for thunder, wouldn't you say?"

"I didn't notice. I was trying to get in out of the rain."

"It's a heller, all right. Ain't a fit night out for man nor bitch."

"Built up a hell of a thirst gettin' here."

"What'll you have, Mr. Long?" Humble Earl asked, and when Longarm named Maryland rye, the bartender nodded and poured a shotglass to the brim. "You know your good drinking, mister."

Longarm tossed back the rye and nodded, feeling the comforting burn of the liquor deep inside.

"A man lives long enough, he's bound to learn something," he said.

Humble Earl nodded and refilled his glass. "*If* he lives long enough. You come in on the ten o'clock, huh?"

Longarm sipped his rye now, and nodded.

"Probably didn't have no dinner," Willis said. He waved his arm. "We boast the finest free lunch west of Denver. Why don't you help yourself?"

"Thanks. That's kind of you."

"Hell, man buys Maryland rye is welcome to belly up to our buffet spread like a hound dog to hot gravy. Our free lunch goes with a nickel beer."

Longarm thanked Humble Earl again. As he turned from the bar, his third shotglass brimming with rye, the bar owner's voice stopped him. Willis spoke in a dead, flat tone that was not intended as a question. "You a lawman, ain't you."

Longarm exhaled heavily and nodded. "You're the second—or third—fellow tonight that recognized me on sight. Is there a smell about me?"

The men along the bar watched coldly and silently, but Humble Earl smiled and shrugged. "A man lives long enough—in Carp—he is bound to learn to recognize lawmen and bounty hunters on sight."

"Oh. You get a lot of them, do you?"

Earl didn't smile. "Buried quite a number over the years. Since the placer mines are playin' out, buryin' you lawdogs is gettin' to be our number-one industry."

"That's right." The customer nearest Longarm nodded emphatically. "They keep comin' in—and we keep buryin' 'em."

"Seems like they don't live long enough to learn," another man said. They nodded and watched Longarm without smiling.

"You fellows have built up quite a hate for the law here in

9

Carp, haven't you?" Longarm inquired.

"Ain't the law. It's what you fellows try to come in here and do that riles us," a man said. The others nodded in silent agreement.

"I see. And what's that?" Longarm said. He didn't bother to smile, either.

"Hell, mister," Humble Earl said, "you sure ain't no mystery to us. You're here lookin' to take in Little Billy Bates. Right?"

Longarm's jaw tightened. "That's right. On a federal warrant."

"Hell. Federal, local, or just some bounty hunter with a wanted flier—you're all the same. You all come in here where you got no right, tryin' to take in Little Billy when you got no chance."

Longarm stared into Humble Earl's tiny eyes for a long moment, then glanced at the taut men nearest him. He grinned at them like a mule eating briars. "I'll just mosey over and make myself a sandwich."

"You do that," Humble Earl said. "You eat hearty."

"Yeah. Might be a long night for you, lawman," one of the barflies said with a smile not meant to be shared. "Or a short one."

"Depending on what you try to do," a fellow beside him said.

"Eat hearty, Long," Humble Earl said again.

Longarm exhaled heavily. "Kind of a last supper, huh?"

Humble Earl Willis nodded seriously. "You might say that."

"You try to take in Little Billy, and bang!—you're dead," a lean cowpoke said, staring at Longarm.

Longarm shook his head, glancing around the room. "Way you fellows talk, this Little Billy Bates must be some fast-shootin' hombre."

Humble Earl shook his head. "I never said that."

"Oh? What did you say?"

"Little Billy Bates has got friends here in Carp, mister. That's all I said."

Longarm had shifted slightly, heading toward the lunch bar. He hesitated, deciding to put a little sanity back into this crazy, storm-struck night. "You people can get yourselves in quite a fix, going against a federal marshal." His tone was mild, but his voice crackled with suppressed fury.

Humble Earl didn't back down. "Look, Mr. Long, Mr.

10

Federal Marshal. Nobody in this here town means to let no outside lawman come in here and molest Little Billy Bates."

Longarm drew a deep breath. It was clear enough what these people meant, but he wanted it out on the table, all cards faceup. "You mean you people—all of you here in this saloon—would keep me from taking in Billy Bates—even if I could?"

"That's what I'm saying, Long." Humble Earl nodded again and swiped at the wet bartop with a damp rag. "You might say protectin' Little Billy Bates is our biggest industry these days. He's the onliest reason men like you git off that westbound. Either they come in here to kill Little Billy to make a gun rep for theirselves, or to collect a few hundred measly bucks on some wanted flier, or to arrest him in the name of Uncle Sam or somebody. But as you can plainly see, Billy is still here."

"And he stays here as long as he wants," the cowpoke said.

Longarm glanced around the muted, smoke-clouded room. A few men played poker, but most of them watched him, stolidly and silently. He couldn't find a friendly face, or even one uncommitted. It was clear these people had backed Little Billy Bates before in his confrontations with the law, and they would do it again. They looked as if they might let Longarm walk out of this place and board the eastbound limited at dawn—if he went alone. He found no cautious faces, either. Not even the threat or certainty of reprisal from Uncle Sam scared these people. He found chilled hatred in every man's face, and no weakness in any woman.

Humble Earl stood smiling flatly behind his bar, and the rest of the townspeople waited, watchful, following Willis's lead.

Longarm sucked in his breath and casually sipped at his rye when casual was the last thing he felt. It was as if somebody were taking dally hitches in his belly. He'd been in tighter spots than this, but the knowledge didn't keep him from feeling ill at ease amid a roomful of folks who'd kill him as casually as they'd step on a bug.

It was unbelievable, the trap he'd walked into, but he knew better than to permit a trace of this to show in his rawboned face. And he was confident of his own skills at his chosen profession. He drank his rye and set the shotglass down on the bar.

"So you see how it is, Marshal," Humble Earl said.

Longarm conceded nothing. He merely shrugged and looked around tentatively. "I'll just fix myself up a sandwich."

As he turned from the bar, a man suddenly stepped out between him and the free-lunch counter.

The fellow was huge, and wore the streaked coat and Levi's of the placer miner. His apelike body spread out from his small head and nonexistent neck to a barrel chest, a potbelly without an ounce of fat in its entire expanse, and keglike thighs. His face was sun-crusted, and his big, callused fists were cracked and dirty.

Longarm didn't know what to expect, but since the big man looked like the town's champion fighter, he set himself for the rush.

It didn't happen. Instead, the big man chewed, working a tobacco cud in his mouth. Suddenly he cupped his battered hat with his hand and spat. A glob of brown phlegm and tobacco juice, splattered between Longarm's boots.

Longarm stood rigid. He waited for the raging waves of laughter, but there was not a sound. Everybody in the room went on watching him. The next move was his, and they knew what it must be.

"Sorry, friend." There was no trace of regret or apology in the big fellow's voice. "But we're practicing for our big to-bacco-spittin' contest, and you're jest standin' right in our way."

"That's right," the fellow siding the potbellied miner agreed. He put his head back and spat toward Longarm. "Got to allow for elevation and windage."

Longarm retreated a couple of steps, but they would not let him retreat peaceably. A third contestant's attempt to outdistance his competitors almost struck Longarm in the thigh. He managed to sidestep it.

Still, there was no laughter in the room, but simply a growing tension. Some of the bystanders glanced slyly at one another now, and grinned covertly.

As a fourth man geared up to spit toward him, Longarm suddenly drew his gun.

The man almost swallowed his cud. The huge miner yelled, "What the hell you doin'?"

Longarm met his gaze levelly, and kept the gun fixed. "Why, shit," he said. "Practice is a great idea. Since it looks

12

like I might be in a shootin' contest, I might as well get in a little practice of my own."

They watched in stunned silence. Before anyone could speak or move, Longarm squeezed the trigger. The Colt .44-40 detonated with thunderous echoes. The sound rattled glasses on shelves behind the bar, and reverberated deafeningly in the enclosed space.

The bullet splintered a floorboard between the big miner's run-over boots.

The miner went toppling backward, swearing. He struck against other drinkers, knocking them over like tenpins.

"Why, you crazy son of a bitch," the miner raged, "you'll kill somebody."

"Sorry." Longarm mimicked the miner's insincere apology. "You fellows just happen to be standing in *my* way."

While men were still straightening up along the bar, Longarm shifted the gun slightly again, moving it in the direction of the second spitter.

He pretended to stare at his Colt. "Sometimes a gun bucks upward, no matter how steady you hold it."

The man yelled, shaking his head and waving his arms: "All right. All right, you loco son of a bitch. You made your point. You don't have to kill nobody."

"I *hope* I don't," Longarm said, and sighed heavily. He did not reholster his Colt for the moment, but stood holding it negligently at his side, in plain sight.

He heard people shifting uncomfortably in their chairs, or retreating a step or two at the bar. He waited, but no one left the saloon, though he thought several men looked as if they devoutly wished themselves anywhere else on earth at this moment, even at home in bed with their own wives.

They had never seen anything quite like him before in Carp. Well, that was fair enough; he'd seldom encountered such a collection of assholes in one place in his life, either.

Longarm shifted his gaze slowly from face to face, from table to table. While he had their attention, there was no sense in letting up on them.

He spoke coldly, his voice shattering the chilly stillness of the garishly lit room. "While I still got my gun in my hand, and you jaspers still got sense enough to know I'll use it—and keep using it till I get what I want—why don't some of you honorable citizens tell me where I can find Little Billy Bates, and we can all get back to our drinking."

People caught their breaths and glanced at each other. Some looked ill, faces ashen and rigid, while others twisted in their chairs as if the seats were suddenly unbearably hot.

"You lookin' for Billy Bates?" A wizened and sun-fried little man spoke from a poker table near the front wall. He sat with a stout woman and three other men over high-stakes, five-card stud.

"That's right." Longarm nodded. "Know where I can find him?"

"You've found him, friend," the little man said in his high-pitched, nasal voice. He stood up slowly. "I'm Billy Bates."

Longarm stared at the road agent, stunned with shock. He didn't know what he'd expected in this weird night, but it wasn't this. Even standing on his tiptoes, Billy Bates didn't come up to Longarm's watchfob.

Chapter 2

"Let me have your gun, Billy," Longarm said. Still holding his own Colt at his side, but ready, Longarm walked between the crowded tables to where Bates stood.

"Ain't got one, Marshal." Billy Bates's nasal whine rose above the whispers in the crowded room. To prove he was clean, Little Billy shoved back his coat, revealing no gunbelt and no holster. He slapped his vest and broadcloth jacket to prove he carried no hideout. With his coat pushed away, Little Billy's torso resembled a gnarled, dry tree stump, with all the life sucked out of it by intensive heat. Dehydrated, he looked as if he weighed less than one hundred pounds in suit and boots, including the flat-crowned black planter's hat he wore cocked over his brow. His eyes resembled those of a hawk, and his nose was beaklike. His thin lips were a taut line, and his jutting chin looked as sharp as a hatchet. Little Billy Bates wasn't much to look at, thin as a drift-fence post, ten times as hard, and a hundred times uglier. His face was like long-dried adobe, seamed with cooked-in lines, and even in the saloon there was habitual squint to his bleached blue eyes. "I don't wear a gun."

"That's right, Marshal." A buxom woman seated beside

15

Billy nodded, placing her hand protectively on the little road agent. "I don't let him wear a gun. You can ask anybody."

"And who are you?" Longarm inquired.

Billy Bates laughed—a twanging, taunting sound, emitted through his beaked nose. "Why, this here is my lady, Marshal. You mean they sent you out here lookin' for me and didn't tell you about my lady? Why, this here is Fanny Fawkes. All you need to know about my lady is right there in her name. Fawkes. Fanny Fawkes. And Fawkes. And Fawkes."

"Now, Billy," the rotund woman protested. Longarm stared at her, impressed by her girth as well as by her obvious devotion to the little outlaw. She weighed maybe a hundred and eighty pounds, though she was only an inch or so taller than her withered lover.

"What's the matter, Fanny?" Billy said. "Ain't you my lady? And you love puttin' out, don't you?"

Her face flushed faintly and she lowered her eyes. "For you, Billy."

"This here's my lady, Marshal." Billy clapped the stout woman on her round shoulder. "Difference between us and most men and women that are together, we care about each other. Don't we, Fanny?"

"You know it, Billy."

Billy nodded, laughing and pleased. "Everybody knows it. Fanny's the one started calling me Master Bates. Years ago. At first I hated it. Then I got so it didn't bother me, 'cause I knew she loved me when she said it. Like Fanny knows I love her when I call her Fishtail Fanny."

"Now, Billy," Fanny said, pawing at him. "You don't have to tell everything you know."

"She knows I love her. She knows I call her Fishtail 'cause Fanny's the best eatin' west of Denver." Billy went off into paroxysms of laughter. Everybody in the room smiled and glanced at each other. "When things go well, I provide Fanny with the best any woman could ask. Don't I, Fanny?"

"You're good to me, Billy," she said.

"And when times are lean, Fanny provides for us, the best way a woman can, bringing in money fast and regular."

"That's all right, Billy," Fanny said. "We don't have to talk about it right now."

"Hell we don't," Billy said. "This here lawdog has got a right to know what he's up against. He's already found out this

16

here town's against him tryin' to take me in. He might as well
know you and me is a team—all the way." Billy nodded emphatically. "Fanny and me live well—whether it's me bringing
in the money, or her. I give her everything she wants when I
can, and she gets me everything I need."

"It's all right, Billy," Fanny said.

Billy turned on her, snarling savagely. "Stop nagging at me,
Fanny. Goddammit, I'll hit you in the tits in a minute." He
looked up at Longarm. "That's one thing Fanny can't stand—
being hit in the tits. But sometimes it's the only way I can git
her attention. I tell you true, the way I feel about a man and
a woman. A man is meant to be the master, and the woman
was plain made to please and satisfy him."

"You know I believe that, Billy," Fanny said. "With all my
heart. I do everything you tell me."

"Except shut up. Shut up now and let me be, less'n you
want to git my fist in your nipples. Goddamn, three things God
shouldn't ax any mortal man to endure: a chafed crotch, a tack
in his shoe, and a backtalkin' woman."

"I just don't want you sayin' too much, Billy."

"You just roll me a smoke, and I'll say what needs to be
said," Billy told her.

"All right, Billy." She took the makings from her oversized
handbag and quietly rolled him a limber cigarette, drawing it
along the tip of her tongue to seal it.

Billy nodded, satisfied. He stared up at Longarm and jerked
his head toward his woman. "I'm a chain-smoker myself,
Marshal—filthy habit, but one I can't break. Can't buy 'em
fast enough." He nodded toward the high-piled butts littering
an oversized ashtray at his side. "Fanny has to roll my cigarettes
for me. Keeps her busy. Keeps her out of mischief. 'Cause my
old fat-ass girl knows iffen she don't have me a coffin nail
ready when I need it, I'll hit her in the tit. Like I say, she can't
take that. But I don't have to hit her very often—she's learned
to roll 'em faster even than I can smoke 'em."

"Looks like you got plenty to be thankful for," Longarm
said.

"That's what I'm tryin' to tell you. I wouldn't live long,
you cage me up where I can't get to Fanny, or she can't get
to me with my smokes and anything else I need. I got to stay
free. For Fanny."

"That's not up to me, Bates," Longarm said. "I got a warrant on you for stealing government property from mail trains and stagecoaches. I take you in as a road agent. The rest is betwixt you and the courts."

"I think we better talk about that," Billy said.

"Nothing to talk about. Only one way to keep from going back with me, Billy—that's murder. You don't want another murder charge on your head, do you?"

"I ain't got none, Marshal. See, that's where you're wrong. Whether I'm a road agent or not, like your warrant claims, has got to be proved in a court of law. You know that. But one thing is sure. I ain't kilt nobody. Hell, I ain't slung a gun in ten years. Give it up when I met Fanny. She kept me so whupped down, I was too weak to pack iron!"

Laughter rolled around the table, where the otherwise silent men watched Longarm relentlessly.

"Somebody's going to have to shoot me, or you're going back with me, Billy. And you better tell your townspeople, you start killing U.S. marshals and you're going to have the army and the federal law in here up to your ass. You can kill me, or one of your good pals can, but they'll keep sending in marshals, and it's all over for anybody mixed up in it."

Little Billy waved his bony hand and laughed. "Come on, Marshal. You got us fellows all wrong. I ain't robbed no stages nor no trains in years. Statute of limitations has run out on ol' Billy Bates, Marshal. And nobody in this here town *wants* to kill you—or any other lawman. Why, we're just ordinary folks here in Carp. Hardworking. Peaceable. But we do stand up for one another, that's all."

Longarm laughed. He looked down at Little Billy Bates, hardly believing what he saw. The famed road agent was nothing like he had expected—in many ways a lot less, in others a hell of a lot more. But one thing was sure. Little Billy was slinging shit by the shovelful right now. Bates had never done a day's work in his life, yet there he sat, poker chips stacked high in front of him, a loving and obedient woman beside him, cocky, arrogant, sneering at his enemies, and probably secretly laughing at his friends.

"Don't make no never-mind to me, Billy. The warrant for your arrest is new and legal, and I mean to carry out its requirements. You can come peaceful, or you can come tough, but you're coming. How you do it—yowling or smiling—that's up to you."

Billy Bates gave Longarm a weasel grin and slouched back in his chair. He fired up one of his cigarettes, took a deep drag, and coughed helplessly. Fanny bent over him, troubled, like a mother hen with her last chick. "When do you mean to take me in, Marshal?" Billy asked finally, dragging on the butt again.

"I figure in the morning," Longarm said. "First train east. No sense delaying."

"Still, morning—that is a long time away, now ain't it?" Billy said, his lips pulled back in smile as treacherous-looking as it was false. "Sit down. There's plenty of time for parley." He jerked his head toward the man seated with his back to the saloon wall. "Hugo, move over. Let the marshal sit with his back to the wall. As anybody can see, he ain't exactly surrounded by friends in here."

Hugo moved over, dragging his cards and chips with him, and Longarm sat down with his back against the wall. He sat with the Colt in his lap, his fist closed upon it. He grinned at Billy. "Your concern is real touching, Bates."

"Hell, I figger you and me will be mighty close before all this here is over, Marshal," the nasal voice said. "I'll do what I can to protect you from these good folks, but hell, I can't guarantee nothing."

"Maybe you better make a few guarantees, Billy," Longarm said in a flat, dead tone.

Billy's head jerked up. "What the hell you talking about?"

"You. You see, I may die, but I figure you'll die first. My gun is fixed on your gut—what there is of it. So I hope none of your friends gets too anxious about your health—"

"Why not?"

"Anybody looks like he's drawing down on me, I'll have to kill you, Billy."

"Now that's a hell of a way to talk," Billy whined.

"But it's the way it is. It's just the way it is. I'm taking you back to Denver. Dead or alive."

"What about my chance in the law courts you was talking about?" Billy protested.

"That's up to you. The warrant calls for me to bring you in. That's all. Dead or alive. I'd just as soon take you back alive. But that's up to you—and your friends. I say to you plain, the first sign of trouble—with anybody—I'm going to plug you."

"Goddamn," Billy said. "I was hopin' you and me could be reasonable about this. But you ain't reasonable. No way. You're plumb loco. Kill-crazy, that's what you are. A cold-hearted son of a bitch."

Longarm shrugged. "Like you said, Billy, I'm not exactly surrounded with friends in here. I didn't plan it this way, but that's the way it's dealt—and I mean to play the cards the way they fall."

A stillness had settled in the room. The air grew fetid and close, but nobody in the place appeared to notice it. The tension was thick enough to cut, with everybody staring at Billy Bates and Longarm, across the poker table from each other.

Billy swallowed at his prominent Adam's apple and glanced about the room. He brought his gaze back to Longarm's face and shook his head. "Now take it easy, friend. You got everybody in here all worried. This ain't no gunslinging town. Nobody's out to kill you. This place is a workingman's settlement. These people are hardworking and tame."

"I hope you're right, Billy. For your sake."

Billy stared up at the old Seth Thomas clock on the saloon wall. It was long past midnight, but no one had left to brave the storm. Everyone watched Longarm and Billy Bates, wondering when the break would come. It was coming, they knew that. There had been lawdogs yowling at Billy's heels before. They were gone, and Billy still ruled the roost around Carp.

Just the same, they were uneasy.

Little Billy grinned reassuringly around the table, his cracked face grimacing. He spoke loudly in his nasal whine. "Well. Looks like Marshal Long here's callin' the cards. Way it looks, it's his deal. He's got us treed for sure." He lifted a hand high and said, "Don't nobody make no fool moves that ain't called for. Mr. Long here means to shoot me, does any of you friends of mine get fractious. Now I've knowed a lot of lawdogs in my time. Some could be reasoned with. Some could be bought at a reasonable price. Mr. Long don't look like he'll listen to nobody. Says he's going to take me back to Denver on the eastbound at daybreak. So why don't we all calm down and jest wait? I mean it's still raining cats and dogs and elephant piss outside. And any way you cut it, no train goes through Carp till dawn. Looks like a long night—for Mr. Long."

"You worry about me too much, Bates," Longarm said.

20

Billy gave him one of his most pleasant, empty, and treacherous smiles. "I ain't worried about you, Marshal. I don't give a shit about you. Why don't we have a few hands of five-card stud?"

"This mean you're fixing to go quiet with me on that limited?" Longarm inquired.

Little Billy grinned at him. "It means just what I said. Fanny believes when you're gonna get raped anyway, you might as well relax and enjoy. You might know about the law business, Mr. Long, but I reckon ain't nobody more expert on rape of one kind or another than my Fanny."

"Now, Billy," the stout woman simpered, "that ain't no way to talk about a lady."

"About my lady it is. Look at her, Marshal. This here beauty is what you want to rip me from, and lock me away from, and deny me. And for what? Few little crimes older than my boots that somebody *says* I committed."

Longarm grinned and shrugged. "Maybe you'll get back to her, Bates, in a few years."

"A few years! You *are* a coldhearted son of a bitch—and likely queer."

Fanny gently touched Billy's arm. "Now, Billy, don't get all riled up. The marshal ain't likely queer, big as he is an' all—"

"You don't know anything about it. If it wasn't for big queers, what would little fairies do? You been around real men so long you don't understand these lah-de-dah boys from Denver, with their limp wrists."

Longarm smiled faintly. "You ain't making me mad, Bates, no matter what you say. Why don't we play stud?"

"We'll play poker when I'm ready to play poker, mister," Billy spat. "You forget this is my town, my people, my card game—and my woman."

Longarm exhaled heavily and said nothing. There was no display of guns, no overt threat, and yet there whirled a great churning in the pit of his belly, for no reason he could explain. It was all too easy—Bates was unarmed, relaxed, content to sit and wait. Wait for what, for hell's sake?

Billy was grinning, leaning across the table again, half sprawled across it, staring up at him, the saffron light playing on his seamed, sun-cured face. The way Billy sat, twisted that way, somehow summoned into Longarm's mind an image of a sidewinder sunning on a mesa—pleasant-looking, easygoing, treacherous. It occurred to Longarm to be doubly alert; Little Billy Bates was likely one of those members of the snake family that didn't rattle before it struck.

"You hear what I said, Marshal?" Billy was demanding in that wheedling tone.

"What was that, Billy?"

"I said if you was a man liked women, you wouldn't even think about trying to take me away from my Fanny for even as long as one night—"

"Robbing the U.S. government was your idea, Billy."

Billy grinned and shrugged. "Hell, if a man can't rob his own government, who *can* he rob? They's fellows on Wall Street and in Washington that make careers and millions out of robbing Uncle Sam."

"When I get warrants for 'em, I'll arrest 'em."

"That's just it, you big son of a bitch. You won't never git no warrants for *them*. They're the big boys, the ruling class, the thieves in expensive suits. An' here you are, trying to take me away from my Fanny when I'd be dead in a week—no, in two days—without her kindly ministrations."

"Why don't we just play cards?" Longarm said.

Billy's voice flared. "Why don't you listen to me, big man, while you got the chance?"

Longarm exhaled heavily. "All right, Billy, what is it you want to say?"

"Look at her, man! I can't no way live without her. She buttons on my shirt for me, and puts on my boots and pulls 'em off at night or when we want a little nap."

"That's interesting as hell, old son, but it ain't got a damn thing to do with robbing trains."

"The hell it don't!" Billy came up abruptly in his chair.

Longarm reacted, his fist grasping the Colt, fixing it on the small moving target across the table.

Billy yelled at him. "Go ahead, big man. Pull that trigger. Kill me. Here. Right now. In front of all my friends. 'Cause if you had the sense of a sick steer, you'd know you'd be killing me by taking me from Fanny. Man, look at her. She was born—and fatted up—just to comfort a man. Ain't that right, Fanny?"

"If you say so, honey."

"My God, Long, you blind? Just look at them tits. Why,

22

her tits are as big as my head. Why, sometimes, playing, she gets my nose stuffed in between them melons and almost suffocates me! But she's got tender tits, so when I bite 'em hard enough, she screams and lets me go—fast."

"You may not get a lot of that in prison," Longarm said. "Anyway, not right at first."

"You heartless son of a bitch! You just don't care how two lovin' people feel about each other, do you?"

"Oh, I care, Bates. It just ain't got a thing to do with me, that's all."

Billy's thin lips twisted. "What the hell you know about it? You're an empty-hearted lawdog, prowlin', sniffin' at shit. What do you know about a woman what can't sleep at night until I've banged her off a couple of times?"

Fishtail Fanny's round face colored brightly, but she spoke with some corroborating pride. "Master Bates has got French blood in him. A lot of it, I swear. I figure he's got to be French. Name is likely French, and he sure likes everything French. Everything." She smiled and lowered her eyes, but she reached over and caressed her lover's lap. "I swear, I tell Billy I'm so fat because I eat him so much."

Billy leaned across the table. "You see, Long, that's what I'm trying to tell you. What do you know about two people who need each other so much? And not just in bed. She needs me to take care of her and tell her what to do."

"Things like going out and whoring for you, Billy?" Longarm inquired.

Billy laughed at him. "There you are, with your straitlaced, old-fashioned ideas about what a lady is. A lady is inside herself. She could whore all day and all her life and still be a lady. A lot of sluts have died with never a prick in 'em. Fanny sells it for money to keep us going when she has to. I ain't heard her complain."

"You'd probably hit her in the tits if she did."

Billy snarled. "That proves how stupid you are. Fanny does what she does for me because she wants to. Ain't that right, honey?"

"That's right, Billy-baby."

"Fanny gives a man his money's worth. She don't cheat nobody no more'n I do. You play cards with me all night, you might get beat bad, but won't be no cheatin', 'less you do it." Longarm saw some of the players around the table nodding in agreement. Billy *was* among friends; he couldn't afford to forget that for one split second.

Billy reached out and caressed Fanny's throat. "For five bucks, a man gits buck-nekkid with Fanny and she gits buck-nekkid too. With her it's easy. Couple buttons, that's all. Hell, Fanny's dressed for business right now." Billy nodded emphatically. "Two buttons. One under her left arm. Other on her left hip. You open that one button under her arm and I swear you git a view you won't match this side of the Grand Tetons—"

"Now, Billy." Fanny smiled in her flushed, shy way.

Billy watched her with devotion glittering in his sun-bleached blue eyes. "She acts shy, but you don't hear her denyin' it. She's one beautiful woman. A whole lot of beautiful woman. And a man gits it all for five bucks. Couple buttons to loosen and she's bare-ass, 'ceptin' for her shoes. And she'll take off her shoes if you ax her to."

"If you ask real polite," Fanny said, giggling, with her head lowered.

"And for that same five bucks, you not only git to look at her—the kind of beauty Rembrandt would have shot his wad over—but you git a ride you plain will recall when you're too old to git a hard-on anymore. And for five extra bucks, Fanny goes 'round the world on you, or gives you a French lesson that makes your eyes bleed."

"Sounds real commendable," Longarm said. "Fanny is a lovely-looking lady, as you say. For a man whose tastes run to curves, I can see how she'd run him out of his mind. And you sell her for five bucks. Don't seem to me you care very much."

"That's how stupid you are, big man. I care. Fanny cares. And her customers care. Five bucks is a lot of money out here, where a man works hard for every damn penny. And five bucks a throw adds up fast. Hell, Fanny can make us a hundred or a hundred and fifty a night—easy—and still lay me good when she comes in from working."

"I admire you, Miss Fanny," Longarm said. "But I don't see how you find time to go to the bathroom."

Fanny's gaze brushed across his. "I don't have to bathe between customers." She put her head back, laughing. "I sweat a lot."

24

Little Billy dealt for five-card stud. He was adept with the cards, slick and smooth, but Longarm could catch no hint of the little man's palming cards or fast shuffling. All these men knew poker; they'd all played their share. It was just that Billy had spent more time at poker tables than anywhere else.

And he was a born gambler. Right now the little road agent was gambling for his own life, but no one could have guessed it by looking at him.

The man beside Fanny—who sat in on the game but did not play—tossed a gold piece in the pot. "I open for twenty."

Everybody stayed, and it cost them, when Little Billy bluffed them with a pair of treys that no one dared pay to see. He laughed at them, a wolfish grin, and raked in the chips. Everything else in Humble Earl's saloon ceased as men and women watched the poker game raptly.

As the silent game progressed through the dark hours of early morning, Longarm cashed his chips a couple of times. He was not sleepy; he felt alert, wide awake. He knew he had to be ready—for what, he had no inkling.

The men around the table hunched over, caught up in the game, hard-faced, sweating, taut with concentration, using all their skills and all the intuition at their command, but Little Billy remained the big winner. There were stacks of chips piled before him that represented a thousand dollars at least.

Longarm had always been proud of his prowess at stud poker, but he had the faint, nibbling feeling that he had been allowed to win only often enough to keep his mind occupied. And it was odd; not one of his winning pots had been at the expense of Little Billy. It was almost as if he were being protected by his fellow cardplayers. By now, Longarm had learned they were the richest men in these parts—the mill owner, ranchers, the holder of the largest placer-mine claim, a shipper. Billy wouldn't sit in with any but rich men. He found no challenge in taking wages from a mine worker.

Billy squirmed in his chair like a hyperactive five-year-old. He was seldom still, twisting, scratching his crotch, feeling his lady's stout leg under the table. His smirking, taunting gaze flickered across the faces of Longarm and the others, touching at one man, then flipping away to another.

The back door of the saloon was shoved open, and rain torrented in shafts and rivulets, swirling in from the alley.

Longarm's heart sank and then beat crazily. His hand closed on the Colt, and he heard Billy laughing at him. "Why, that's just Crazy Charlie Wilkes. Works in the livery stable, shoveling horseshit. Comes in every morning this time for his free-lunch breakfast."

Longarm exhaled, seeing the fissures of pink, false dawn in the rainswept sky before Crazy Charlie Wilkes got the rear door closed.

"Jesus, look at that rain," somebody said.

"Ever see such a flood?"

"Water's up three or four feet in the livery stables," Crazy Charlie Wilkes said.

Billy Bates grinned crookedly. "Looks like the eastbound will be delayed this morning—even more than usual."

"Limited never has been on time through here since it started running."

Billy Bates slouched back in his chair, watching Longarm with a grin of triumph.

That grin made Longarm's decision for him. Though he didn't know exactly how, he was certain the unarmed Billy Bates felt he held high cards in this deadly game between them. It was to let Billy know who was in command.

Longarm glanced negligently toward the old Seth Thomas, wheezing on the saloon wall. It was almost 6:00 A.M. "All right, Billy. On your feet. We'll go on over to the depot and wait for the limited."

"Are you full of shit?" Billy said. "Why sit over there? We can be comfortable right here. They'll let us know when the train comes—if it makes it."

"Just the same, we'll wait over there." Longarm stood up and held the Colt in plain sight of Billy and all his friends. He tilted his head. "If you people have got the brains of billygoats, you'll stay out of this. You'll stay here in the saloon. You'll let me handle it. That way nobody gets hurt."

"That makes sense," Billy agreed.

"Glad you see that," Longarm said. He gestured with the gun. "Let's go, Billy."

"Why should we go over there and wait in the rain?" Billy protested,

"There are a lot of reasons, Billy, all of them good. But the

26

only one that matters a damn is that I say it's what we're going to do. And that's all the reason you need."

It was Little Billy Bates's suggestion that Crazy Charlie string ropes from the veranda post outside Humble Earl's saloon, across the boiling cataract of Main Street to a post at the freight depot.

When the livery stable worker had knotted the lariat around a freight platform post, he stood in the rain waving his hat back and forth. He was like a rain-battered shadow in the dim morning.

Billy got up quietly. Carrying a sun parasol, Fanny got up too. "You don't need to go out in that storm," Longarm told her.

"She goes," Billy said tersely.

Longarm shrugged. As long as Billy went quietly, he was satisfied.

Longarm let Billy and Fanny walk ahead of him to the front door of the saloon. There he took up his sodden carpetbag. He touched at the clasp, then decided against putting handcuffs on a man who barely came up to his watch chain.

Longarm pushed back the folding doors. He retreated slowly through the batwings, checking the porch for any possible Bates confederates. The wind and rain slashed at him like machetes, but the dim street was deserted, a boiling tempest racing toward the Meadow Valley wash and the Colorado beyond.

When Billy and Fanny came out the front door, Fanny opened her parasol. Wind and rain whipped it to tatters in seconds. Swearing, she ripped at the flimsy cloth.

Before they reached the edge of the veranda, already drenched, at least a dozen townies, two or three saloon women among them, came through the front door.

Longarm stopped where he was. "You people get back inside. Stay out of this."

The townies stared at him, cold and unblinking.

Longarm swore. "All right, goddammit. You people want to do it the hard way, you got it. You can go back to Denver three ways, Billy: dead, wearing ankle irons and handcuffs all the way, or playing cards like gents. That's up to you."

The rain slamming at him so he had to put his legs apart to brace himself against its force, Billy faced his friends. He gave them one of his crinkled smiles. "Why don't you folks go on back into the bar? No sense seeing me going away

27

humiliated, wearing ankle irons and cuffs."

"We can stop him, Billy," somebody said. Shocked, Longarm realized it was a woman, a faded-haired blonde.

"But that's just it. I don't *want* you to stop him. He's a horse's ass, but he has got the federal government behind him. They'll get you people for trying to help me—and I figger this big turd will shoot me, the first move one of you folks makes."

"You got it figured just right," Longarm told him.

Billy shrugged and spread his hands. "There you are. This is the kind of gun-crazy, government-backed loco we're dealing with. It ain't worth it. I'll be back. You'll see. You folks just mosey on back to the bar and wait. Tell you what—after my train leaves, Fanny will come back over and help you fellows forget—at five bucks a throw." He laughed disarmingly. "And don't nobody try to take advantage of Fanny's good nature, neither, because I will be back—and I never forget a wrong or a debt or a deadbeat."

The townies hesitated, then retreated as far as the door. They crowded in the doorway, their gazes fixed on Fanny, Longarm, and Little Billy Bates.

Holding his gun ready in his right fist, Longarm backed to the edge of the porch, caught the rope, and tested it. Rain pounded him. He backed away slowly, clutching the lariat. The raging water lashed about his legs with fearful force. "All right, let's go. Billy first."

Grinning, ducking his head against the pummeling of the rain, Billy caught the lariat and eased himself through the water. He never took his grinning gaze off Longarm's face.

Behind Billy, Fanny Fawkes staggered, plodded, fell, and swore, blowing water from her face. She used her stripped parasol as a cane. Billy didn't even bother glancing over his shoulder at her.

Longarm saw that the townies had come back out on the veranda of Humble Earl's saloon. But none of them had ventured out into the raging torrent of Main Street. What the hell, as long as they kept their distance.

His back touched the boards of the freight platform. He stepped up on it and Billy scrambled up behind him.

Fanny floundered, trying to pull herself up from the rushing water. Billy ignored her. Longarm wanted to help the puffing,

28

arm-flailing fat woman, but he knew better than to take his eyes off Billy.

Fanny managed at last to pull herself up on the wet freight platform. People yelled encouragement from across the river-like thoroughfare.

The whistle of the eastbound limited shrilled, piercing through the thunder and rain.

"Goddamn," Little Billy swore. "Wouldn't you know it? That fuckin' train is early for the first time in history."

Longarm sighed as if he had been holding his breath for at least ten minutes. His chest ached, his throat burned. He relaxed slightly, peering through the gray sheets of rain in the fading darkness.

He never relaxed enough for a sucker punch. He'd been in the business too long for that. When Bates shifted his weight, turning on the slippery platform, Longarm stiffened and stepped back, putting his legs apart to brace himself.

He was aware of everything, the people crowding into the street in front of the saloon, the swirling water, the way Fanny stood with her skeletal parasol, her sopping clothes clinging to her obese form, exaggerating every plane and hillock.

Too late, Longarm jerked his arm up to ward off the blow he never saw coming. Bates didn't strike with his fist. His fast, solid, flying kick caught Longarm just under his left ear, sending him reeling back in the cascading rain.

The hundred pounds of Bates's body were after him like crazed wasps; the little man used his feet like fists. One kick caught Longarm in the throat, immobilizing him.

He emitted a howl of agony that put lights on in every window in the rain-blanketed town, but none was so bright as the flare that erupted, exploded, burned, and blossomed like Roman candles against the crown of his skull.

For a long moment his nerve centers were paralyzed. His sixgun dropped from fingers that would not obey him, and fell into the swirling waters of the street.

Vaguely he heard Fanny screaming, exhorting her man to victory. "Git him, baby," Fanny yelled. "Git him good!"

Longarm felt Bates's feet, like mindless fists driven into his groin, his belly, his solar plexus, his kidney, and, as he fell, over and over into his face.

Longarm was aware of Fanny standing above him, her face

29

wild, screaming like a banshee. Beyond her, Crazy Charlie Wilkes jumped up and down, slavering. The crowd plunged out of the saloon and plodded through the water toward the station.

Pain erupted inside Longarm's skull as he went slamming against the wall of the depot. He heard the ravening howls of the townies, the frenzied laughter that gushed out through Fanny's full lips.

Shaking his head to clear it of spiders drowning in their own cobwebs, Longarm felt Billy kick him mercilessly in the chest. Gasping for breath, Longarm staggered, but refused to fall.

Baying like a frustrated coyote, Little Billy hurled himself upon Longarm, arms about his waist, dragging him down. Billy suddenly bit Longarm's balls, savagely, as a vicious dog might tear at another animal's vitals.

Weakly, Longarm struck at Billy's head, forcing him back. He twisted then, and fell facedown. Billy's boot heel caught his forehead. The boot toe smashed into his cheek. Blood ran from Longarm's ripped mouth.

Behind them, the herd of townspeople, grinning, pressed forward, yelling.

"Kill him. Kill him, Billy."

"Kill the sumbitch."

"You got fifty witnesses you acted in self-defense, Billy."

Longarm heard nothing clearly after that. There was the surging of blood in his temples, the salty taste of the blood spurting like wine inside his mouth.

He lay still, trying to clear his mind enough to act. But when he moved, he felt the bite of the tip of Fanny's parasol against his left eye. "You move, sweetheart," Fanny said from above him, "and you lose that eye."

When Longarm stirred, Billy's boot crashed again into his crotch. Longarm went spinning out into space, where he didn't even feel the rain.

From an eternal distance, he heard the bloodthirsty howls of the mob. "You got him now, Billy. Finish the sumbitch."

Dazed, Longarm lay still, stomped into a strange kind of waking unconsciousness. He could hear the crowd, but he could not see them anymore. He knew Fanny's parasol was thrust hard upon his eyeball, but strangely there was no pain. All the pain in his body was centered in his burning loins. He thought he would throw up, but he couldn't even do that.

He was barely aware of Little Billy moving over him swiftly, removing his weapons and wallet along with the warrant and every piece of Longarm's identification.

Billy stood up. He kicked Longarm in the crotch again, but Longarm fooled him. He was too near dead to feel the pain. He was aware of Billy, Fanny, and Crazy Charlie rolling him over the side of the platform and into the muddy rush of the flood. There was a hell of a splash, but Longarm didn't even feel it.

Chapter 3

Longarm was vaguely aware of being hurled along like a log in the rushing current of the Meadow Valley Wash. He knew he should try to aid himself, but at the moment he was helpless, carried along in the violent, stewing waters.

What he was truly conscious of was his own life passing in review behind his eyes. Moments, memories, and images flashed there on currents of short-circuited pain. There was no comfort, pleasure, or even excitement in this recounting of his existence. For no good reason at all he kept seeing the bald-headed, pink-faced, bushy-browed visage of Chief Marshal Vail, for hell's sake.

What was Billy Vail doing in a terminal replay of his life? If he had to see anything, why not the Californian Mexican doll, Felicidad Vallejo? Or little Clarita, down in Mina Cobre, Arizona Territory? Or the tattooed lady, Minerva, in the circus sideshow? Or Roping Sally, long dead now? But Chief U.S. Marshal Vail? That didn't make good sense; it gave a drowning man no motive for living at all.

And yet that was what he kept seeing: Billy Vail's face, his office, his desk, and his arms flailing in the air. Well, at least

Billy Vail was unchanged in this fouled-up recounting of a misspent life.

The sound of Vail's voice was loud and clear, as were the slap of his open hand on his desktop, the clacking clatter of the newfangled typewriter from the outer office, the crack of Vail's boot heels on the highly polished but uncarpeted office flooring. Vail never let Longarm forget that his government grade didn't entitle him to rugs on the floor, for Christ's sake—you just think on how petty those goddamn bureaucrats in Washington are.

"Why, it's a lead-pipe cinch," Chief Marshal Vail's voice thundered in Longarm's ears, causing pain all the way to the backs of his legs. "A goddamn piece of cake. German chocolate cake, with icing an inch deep and sweeter than virgin piss."

Longarm slouched in the one comfortable chair in Vail's office, the red morocco-upholstered armchair.

"I don't know why it is, Chief," Longarm said, "but every time you promise me a piece of cake, my guts start to turn over and the hairs rise up on the back of my neck."

"Just jumpy, that's all. Shit, here I am offering you a vacation, and you're bitching."

"I've been on your vacations. Where is this Eden you're sending me now? In what part of God's country?"

Billy Vail clopped over to his wall map and jabbed his broken-nailed index finger at a pencil-circled area in a desert that Longarm recognized as the godless wastes above Boulder Canyon.

"Boulder Canyon!" The protest burst across Longarm's lips. "That's godforsaken Paiute country. I know Boulder Canyon—lizards, sidewinders, and buzzards. People call it the far corner of nowhere. And they avoid it like the plague."

"I admit it is open federal land—"

"You bet your ass it is. And 'open federal' is bureaucratic doubletalk for desert wastes nobody wants. Why in hell would you be sending me down there into Boulder Canyon?"

"I'm not. Goddammit, just keep your shirt on." Vail pawed through his stacks of paperwork marked *urgent* from Washington. Vail was a horseman saddled to a desk, and he was going to flab. There was still hardness in his voice and steel in his gaze. At least fifteen years older than Longarm, Vail wore his ill-healed scars like ribbons of valor from long-ago and half-forgotten violence. He'd never fallen victim to any man he went up against. But he admitted he was fighting now the one foe he could never hope to outwit, overcome, or change: age. Age had thrust him behind this pinewood desk, out of harm's way. Balding, desk-shackled, he hated going to lard in belly and jowls. He felt like he ought to be out on these cases; he'd learned how to handle them, the hard way. But once he knew all the tricks of the trade, they'd kicked him upstairs, to safety and unceasing boredom. "Hell, Long, I set this case aside for you my own self."

"Now I got cold sweats."

"I know you been getting roughed up around the edges some. Nothing like the crap we took in the old days, but enough."

Longarm thumbed a slow-healing gun wound in his side and grimaced. "Enough."

"Shit, man, in my day we carried so much lead we clanked when we walked."

"And now it's settled in your ass. What's going on?"

"You ever heard of Carp?"

"Is that something or somebody?"

"It's a little mining town." Vail jabbed his map again. "Right here, about twenty miles up from Las Vegas."

"Where in hell is Las Vegas?"

"Las Vegas is a settlement where the UP stops to jerk water for its locomotive. Not much there—a spring surrounded by a cluster of railworkers' shanties, a general store, and a saloon."

Longarm lit up a two-for-a-nickel cheroot and grinned coldly. "And that's the big town near Carp, eh?"

"Carp's where you're going. A good day's ride to the west of that Boulder Canyon you despise so. Carp's on a seasonal creek called Meadow Valley Wash, a kind of wet-weather stream between Meadow Valley and the Mormon ranges. When it runs, it spills into the Colorado."

"Mining country," Longarm muttered. "Ranges are all tilted fault blocks, with a few juniper and pinyon. Country all around it is desert, full of sagebrush. Flat-top plateau all around barren wastes. Cold in winter. Hot as hell in the summer. You picked a lovely spot for my vacation."

"You're in quick. You're out quick. You go in on the night limited westbound, and you catch the morning limited eastbound—"

"Wait a minute, Billy. Back up. Haven't you forgotten

something? What do I have to do to earn this overnight vacation in paradise?"

"Hell, you got to expect to do a *little* something to earn a hundred bucks a month and expenses, for God's sake. You got any idea what the average workingman makes an hour right now?

"All right, Billy. So there is a *little* something you expect me to do in Carp?" Longarm prompted.

Vail nodded, but then waved his arm negligently. "A warrant. You're to pick up a punk that's been hiding out in Carp. Road agent. Stole some government shipments. Never been caught. But we know he's down there. And we want him."

"I just ask him polite and he comes along quiet, huh?"

"Almost. He has no record for carrying or using guns. No murders charged to him. Like I say, he's just a punk. Does say he's known to have a hair-trigger temper, but nothing to worry about. In on one train, out on the next. Hell, if facing felons is dangerous, this is a picnic. You should hardly get your feet wet."

As usual, Chief Marshal Vail was wrong again. His piece of cake was inedible, and his desert was a flash flood. *My feet are wet, Billy. All the way up to my ears my feet are wet, and I'm earning my princely pay, Chief, every goddamn penny of it . . .*

The flood hurled him about as if he were a small branch, slapping him toward its inundated banks when it rose in spuming swells against them, and then whipping him along toward the far shore.

The river swirled, eddied, and whipped back on itself under the diminishing downpour. It wound, unchecked, uncontrolled, and uncontrollable through drowned meadows of reeds and sodden willows. Elders heavy with mud, bent and ripped from their stands, were carried along with roots exposed on the beige-colored surface, past sandy banks where cottonwoods toppled, uprooted. The course seemed mindless, and yet the flood fled onward, downward through the trackless deserts, the narrow gorges in upthrust faults, racing toward the Colorado and across incredible distances and forgotten lands to the sea.

There were no buildings or structures being carried along on its surface; these wild waters coursed down from lonely hills and lost ranges.

Longarm struck against unnamed and unnameable sub-merged objects. Whether they were animals or trees or drowned human beings, he would never know. For a long time he was barely aware of anything that was happening to him.

The flash flood ripped its way across this waste where there was no sign of man, life, or habitation.

There was a chance that the thrust of water would carry him to some sandbar or high knoll, or into a hammock of juniper, but it did not happen. He was bobbled along on the crest of the water, in the boiling flow of the swollen wash.

Time went unmeasured. The tide carried Longarm so swiftly and easily that he may as have well been rudderless in an irresistible undertow. Crazily, wildly, and rapidly it whirled him around and around, as if every twist of the creek were a boiling cataract, sweeping him almost to one shore and then to the other. The battering downpour waned. Sunrise burst, delayed, a blazing cerise and yellow fire burning away the low-hanging thunderclouds. Cranes and storks and hawks flitted in close to the swollen waters and then were whipped away on the wind, and range buzzards rose from their rocks and caught the drafts in the strange and smoking sky. He drifted on, help-less. Before the rain ceased he had been whipped into larger, merging streams and hurled along faster through black eddies, only to be thrown again into the furious flux of savage waters.

Longarm's unconsciousness was broken at first by strange periods when he half woke, vaguely aware of extreme chill, of paralysis in his hands and in his mind, of acute pain in his groin and chest and legs, of hotly persistent discomfort, and even of half-heard sounds and sights and memories that troubled him, while they eluded him.

He did not realize how long it was before he became aware of what had happened to him, and where he was, and how slim were his chances of survival.

He whipped his head upward in panic. The water rushed around him, flailing at him and threatening to drown him. He managed somehow to breathe, but he didn't know how or why.

With his head upthrust, Longarm returned to consciousness, awake but sick and aching, and helpless in the fury of the flood tide. The eastern horizon, red and lavender now, told him it was daylight. He swore in his agonized and helpless misery. Somehow he could crab his head upward often enough to gasp for life-saving breath. He must have done that ever since he had been thrown into the water, but he had no conscious memory of any of it.

He fought at the gushing water as much as he could, but his arms seemed leaden and useless. Gasping, he looked around in the blaze of morning light, trying to get his bearings. The rain had stopped, but the flood had risen and was still rising, with the cascading creeks and gullies emptying the ranges and mesas and plateaus into the rivers. He had been carried a long way, he had no reasonable idea how far.

There was no sign of life on any side of him. The waters had coursed into a mighty trough that tunneled through the wilderness, but there was only the emptiness of barren plains beyond the cresting waters.

I'll kick my way to the shore, he told himself. *I'll grab on to something and pull myself out of this wild water before I drown. God knows, I'm far past half drowned now.*

He saw weeds and small trees growing along the new-made banks of the stream, but he was whipped past them at incredible speed. Terror flooded through him. Only God knew how fast he was being battered along in this mill race to nowhere. He saw the high knolls, the safe havens with weeds and rocks to cling to, but they went rushing past as if he were aboard a runaway locomotive on the steepest downgrade.

He ordered his legs to kick against the thick, plunging water. He bit back a yell of helpless horror. His legs and arms hung like broken limbs from his body, and he was carried along, unable to break the grasp of the current. Hell, he couldn't even make his body respond to orders from his mind. Helplessly he spun, watching the shore race past.

Dragged down by the weight of his clothes and buoyed only by the force of the surging tide, he faced two facts: He had been kept on the surface by the speed of the water, and it was only a matter of time until the weight of his soaked and mud-clotted clothing would drag him down in some eddy where his forward impetus would not support him.

He struck his shoulder against a boulder submerged in the flow, and bounced out to meet the center of the current. As soon as that blindingly swift motion caught him, he was uplifted and his face raised to the open air. The speed made him dizzy, as if he were drunk, and even though he knew the overwhelming odds were that he would drown, he felt exhilarated.

He gasped in the sweet, dank smell of water and uprooted

land carried on the damp breezes. In the drunken giddiness of being twirled and whirled along, he began to lose his terror in a kind of passive serenity and acceptance. The horror and fear left his mind, and the gloom lifted. He hated like hell to die, but he accepted it. He was going to drown in this deluge. The only question left now was *when?*

This lethargy was a totally unfamiliar emotion for him, and yet he spun in that wide, overflowing river, conscious of this odd, peaceful sensation of being borne along, unable to help himself, and too exhausted and stunned to care anymore. It was almost like tasting a strange, wild sense of freedom.

The blaze of the desert sun broiled his eyes and cooked his head. Now that the rain had ceased, the stunning heat sizzled in the flooded desert wasteland.

The heat restored some feeling in his body, and baked out knots of the paralyzing agony. He didn't begin to think he would live again yet, but deep inside him he felt a faint pang; he wanted to live.

On his back and squinting against the sun, he saw herons and bitterns and other waterfowl lumbering in close along the banks. There was only the thunder of the cascading water in the strange, hypnotic silence of the desert. Like an eerie, enveloping net, the silence seemed to blanket everything, even the maddened flood.

The sun, painfully searing as it was, returned some strength to his arms. He realized why he had seemed paralyzed. It was the numbing cold, dispelled now slightly by the sunlight.

He kicked his feet, at first experimentally. Then he flailed his arms about, simply trying to steer himself in the racing swells.

Ahead of him he saw a sloping bank, where a man could climb to safety once he broke the terrible pull of the current. A few stunted junipers and clumps of sagebrush seemed to offer something to cling to. The summit of the bank was twenty or thirty feet above the rising crest of the flood, and beyond it Longarm could see high and dry plateaus, burning gold and bronze in the sun.

He fought with all his strength. With a sense of victory, he felt himself crossing the flood crest, at a long angle to be sure, and still at breathtaking speeds.

When he came close to the swiftly receding shoreline, he clutched frantically at a clump of sage. The brush ripped free

39

from the wet soil and he was thrown over and over, out into the tunnel of the current again.

For a long time, then, he lay prostrate on the foamy surface, twisting his head only enough to breathe. He panted, exhausted and in pain. His muscles ached and his hands were torn.

Breathing wildly through his open mouth, he stared at the broken, high faults on both sides of the creek. At least he had learned one thing: he would pick a flatter area in which to try to escape the tide. He was going to have to fight his way into some natural eddy formed by boulders or fallen logs if he was to have any chance of crawling out of this cascading stream.

He turned his head in time to see the conelike, jagged crowns of sleek river boulders directly ahead. He swam frantically, kicking his legs, but the force of the current dashed him against the rocks.

Pain exploded through his skull, and he felt his senses reeling. He lay on the water, aware that his skull was bleeding, aware of the flame of the sun and his helplessness against the speed and power of the deluge.

The surge of the water increased suddenly and he spun along, unable to steer himself or even to stay upright in the swelling whirlpools.

He was swept far out into a wide trough where the speed of the current was doubled and tripled. The shore was no longer close or friendly. The thunder of pounding, merging cataracts of streams from the ranges was deafening.

This had to be the Colorado. He was being thrown and slapped along in the great river at flood crest.

A juniper log, ten feet long and six feet around, bounded past like a toothpick on the surface. In panic, he watched the log race past. If he was to stay afloat in the Colorado, he needed a craft, he needed that log.

His cut, burning hands closed on a jagged limb. His fingers tightened. The log didn't slow in its flight, or even turn with his weight, but he was able to hang on.

Longarm managed to slip his arms about the log, secured by the hook of the broken limb. He locked his arms and threw one of his legs across the log as if riding a bucking bull.

With his head resting on the log, the bark biting into his flesh, he panted and grinned tautly. He was still alive—and headed downriver in the Colorado.

Only God knew where he was; only God knew where he was going; and right now, only God cared.

Longarm was too busy being thankful he was still alive and breathing.

When Longarm lifted his head from the log after a long time, he saw the mighty river and valley lost in immense loneliness. One thing he knew for sure: he was deep in that godforsaken wilderness the bureaucrats called "open federal land."

The silence and the sun beat down on him. He felt cooked and broiling in his own sweat. A luminous and almost blinding yellow light bounced off the rising flood waters. It seemed to him that the sun had crested and moved to his right, overspreading the plains to his west with vivid and nameless colors.

Some distance ahead, the swollen river snaked widely around a high slate knoll. Above and beyond it rose mountain peaks and hills lost in barren ranges. Southward, around that sharp turn, the river flushed through a spillway between close, sheer cliffs.

He rode the log like an overturned canoe now. The buoyant log, driven along on the current, sent him forward swiftly. As he passed between the narrow walls of the canyon, the sun seemed to fade, the world darkened, and the muddy river began to turn a strange, rosy hue.

He saw gray sage scaling the sheer wall of the canyon, and the blue shadows deepened as he descended into the rocky gorge. *One good waterfall,* he thought, *and you've had it, old son. No more Maryland rye, no more pretty-smelling ladies.*

The increasing speed of the river warned him that rapids and maybe some bottomless spill lay ahead.

He clutched the log tighter, helpless to halt or turn it. The scarred walls reared brown and brazed and shadowed to the broken crests, where golden tips of the sun shone or a single juniper crouched jauntily on the high rims.

The walls narrowed and the water whitened. The log danced insanely, as if trying to throw him.

The log went plunging into the rapids. It struck submerged boulders and bounced off lightly. It whipped all the way around. It caught itself on two hidden slate reefs and hung for a long breathless moment before it was ripped free and hurled through the white, misting spume.

41

His arms were battered and bleeding, torn on sharp rocks, but Longarm held on. It seemed to him that his one chance to survive these rapids was to ride the log. He locked his ankles about it, he clasped his arms around it. He hung on and he prayed, between swear-words strung together as he'd never used them before in all his misspent life.

The log rolled and Longarm was carried along under the spewing, gushing surface. The log struck hidden boulders head on, and almost jarred him loose. When he had been spun, jostled, whipped, and battered until he felt he could no longer endure it, the log went skidding free of the rocks and white water.

He drifted around a bend and into a long pool that was rain-swollen and swift-moving, but almost as smooth as a pond after the white rocks and rapids.

Trembling, he hung on, aware of the darkening shadows of the canyon walls reflected on the rose-tinted surface of the river. The sky that he could see between the sheer walls turned drab, and then smoky green in the twilight. The silence in the canyon deepened and a distant star shone palely. Twilight ebbed. Darkness settled over the swift-moving stream, and the night tide raced, hurrying, shadowy, and as still as a cemetery. Even the deafening thunder of flash flooding added its own kind of silence to the unnatural stillness.

As the remote stars glowed and brightened, the deep chasm cut by the river blackened and yet took on sharp, definable shapes. The dim, vague outlines of the walls shone with ebony night, and beyond them loomed the darker crests of far mountains. He rode the log through the thunderous silence of the canyon. From time to time he tried to turn the log or steer it against the fury of the tide. When he grew tired of fighting, he lay and rested upon the log and drifted with the current. The night chill and the danger ahead brought cold, prickling tingles across the nape of his neck. It was impossible not to be scared in the awesome silence and impenetrable blackness and the threat of the unknown just around the next bend in the river, yet he felt excitement as much as fear. He was still alive!

When the night settled and the last wisps of desert heat were blown away on spume-damp mists, Longarm was assaulted by unbearable desert cold.

The night chill clutched at him on the log, seeping into his back and legs and shoulders through his sodden clothing. Even the raging water was slightly warmer than the wind. His teeth chattered, his body shuddered, and he felt the debilitating paralysis of cold attacking his arms and legs.

Hold on, old son! he warned himself. He'd been only half conscious as he'd floated out of Carp on the Meadow Valley Wash, paralyzed with cold and pain. Now, if he lost feeling in his legs and arms, he could kiss goodbye to his speeding, bucking juniper log. It was no yacht, but it was better than fighting every second simply to breathe.

There was one way he knew to fight the cold. He had to think about something else. It seemed to him that the ranges and cliffs on both sides of the river widened and that he drifted rapidly out upon open wastelands again. But it was too dark and there was no way to be sure. And out here, the desert chill intensified.

He forced himself to remember Carp and Little Billy Bates and Fishtail Fanny Fawkes and all the dead-eyed townspeople who watched the little road agent stomp the lawman into unconsciousness and then toss him like debris into the flash-flooding creek.

Remembering the little son of a bitch helped. Rage stirred the blood pumping in veins and arteries, and anger kept him clinging to his bobbing, speeding log. He wondered how long it would be before Chief Marshal Vail sent another deputy marshal into Carp looking for Little Billy and for his missing officer?

He pitied the poor unlucky bastard who drew the assignment to come to Carp looking for him and Bates. There was slight chance the new deputy would live to take Bates out. He winced ruefully at one reason why he was out here lost in a lost world: overconfidence. Why shackle a little fellow who barely came up to his chest? Who ever looked less lethal or dangerous than skinny, unarmed Master Bates?

He shuddered, only partly from the deepening chill. Well, his swaggering self-confidence had brought him here. Where was he? He had no idea; this wild, uninhabited land was trackless, empty, and deadly. This river could yet be his unmarked grave.

There was practically no chance that anyone would ever find him. Nobody outside Carp knew what had happened to him, and nobody in the town cared, or would talk about it. What chance was there that any man in Carp would tell the truth, even if questioned?

He could almost hear the unanimous answering of the entire population. They hadn't known the stranger was a lawman. Some unknown bushwhacker had attacked him, and the marshal was last seen floating away, either dead or unconscious, in a flash flood.

Teeth clattering and cold numbing his body, Longarm swore. He knew now how the lawmen and bounty hunters ahead of him had failed in their missions to Carp. Backshot at night. Knifed in a dark alley. Ambushed. Buried in the limitless sagebrush plains, and no way to connect Little Billy Bates with any disappearance.

Longarm shivered helplessly with rage and bone-numbing chill. He forced himself to see the way Carp had lied about the missing lawmen to save Bates's worthless carcass. As far as they knew, the lawman, or bounty hunter, had been unable to find Billy and had ridden out. Who knew what had happened to him? Maybe the Paiute had eaten his horse. Some of the tribes may have eaten both horse and rider, and parts of his saddle. Hell, who knew?

Longarm quivered, feeling his legs go numb. Above him a million bright stars glittered sharply against the dark dome of heaven. All around him the gloomy wastes were black with impenetrable shadow. The banks of the river showed only faintly.

He was one more lawman who had been sent to Carp. One more missing man. How many before him had been written off as missing or dead?

Well, it was a part of the job; it went with the territory; it was a chance a lawman took—to disappear abruptly without a trace, to be abandoned as "missing," as he would be.

The intense agony of the cold lanced through Longarm like swords of ice. He felt his hands slipping, his arms losing their grip on the log, and he was helpless to grasp it.

The whirling vortex whipped the log around and Longarm was flung from it as easily as a bug.

Wildly he grasped at the rough bark of the juniper trunk. Pain burned through his hands, but the log slipped beyond him. It was borne swiftly away on the rushing tide.

Chapter 4

From somewhere, Longarm heard the whiplash snap of rifle
fire and the instantaneous thump of lead in the sand, inches
from his head.

He jerked upward in a reflex movement, blasted out of
exhausted sleep. The bullet was so close that brown dirt spurted
against his face.

Whoever it was had placed a rifle slug between Longarm's
outstretched arms. He lay sprawled on the bank of the river,
his boots only inches from the lapping water.

He crouched, his fingers digging into the dust, waiting for
the gunman to pump a second cartridge into that rifle chamber
and finish him off.

Seconds ticked away. Longarm thought about grabbing for
his Colt .44-40 in his cross-draw rig and trying to protect
himself, but Little Billy Bates had taken his Colt as well as the
double-barreled hideout he wore in his vest pocket on the other
end of his watch chain.

Longarm exhaled slowly through his parted lips, afraid to
move and afraid to stay where he lay on the damp riverbank.
The finishing shot didn't come, though Longarm knew the
rifleman was standing somewhere above him in the rose-lit

brightness of daybreak. The intense clarity of the sky heightened the sharp and ragged sihouettes of distant sheer walls of buff sandstone. The sun glittered on the quiet river and lay a sheen across a strangely green and verdant valley.

Just as Longarm was about to credit the ambusher with sense enough not to waste ammo on a half-dead stranger, a man's voice called, "I could have put that bullet in your head, mister. The next one goes there, Gentile. Unless you go back into that river now, you are a dead man."

Longarm's cracked, swollen eyelids opened painfully and slowly to a wan, purple desert daybreak. The rising sun warmed him and flamed deeply into his mind.

He raised his head again, cautiously. "Wait a minute, you jackass," he said. "I'm half drowned now. I go back in that river, I'm a goner for sure."

"Drowned or dead from a bullet," the unseen man called, "it is the same with me."

"What you got against me?"

"I don't need to have anything against you, or for you. You are a stranger. A Gentile stranger. We don't need the likes of you here. We don't want you here."

Wincing at the man's unyielding tone, Longarm tensed, awaiting the next rifle slug. "Can't we talk this over?"

"What is there to say, stranger? You, Gentile, have invaded our land. We have made a garden of arid wilderness. We won't have Gentiles like you coming in to take it from us."

"I don't want your land, mister. But I been through hell. I just beat a watery grave. Somehow I would like to go on living—at least temporarily. I'm even crazy enough to want to know the reason why I am to die."

"I told you," the man said in his relentlessly flat and righteous tone, "you are a stranger. We do not permit strangers in Alamut."

Alamut? For a taut moment, Longarm thought he might still be in some nightmare. He had never heard that name before on any town along the Colorado.

"You take me in for one hour, mister. Sell me a horse—I'll have to send you the pay for it—and I'll be out of here so fast you'll forget you saw me."

The strange, thick voice hardened further. "You talk with the glib tongue of the Gentile. But I do not trust you. I warn you for the last time—go back into that river."

46

"The hell with that," Longarm decided. "If I'm going to die, I'll die dry. I'm not going back in that river, mister. If you want me dead, you'll have to kill me."

He heard the sharp intake of breath from the unseen gunman. The fellow wanted to be rid of him; he mistrusted strangers and Gentiles. This meant he must be part of the Mormon tribes that had spread out over the flat lands and ranges west of Salt Lake. Some had splintered off from the Chosen People; others wanted to continue with polygamous marriages after both the Church and the federal government had outlawed the practice. Still others were looking for new lands, for places where they could live, worship, and rule their own in their own view of Mormon law. This man, whoever he was, dreaded to use a gun to kill another human being; otherwise that first bullet would have splatted into Longarm's skull.

"Don't force me to kill you, Gentile," the unseen man said. "I do not want your blood on my hands. But I will not have you in our holy lands. You have gone against God. You go against me. I will kill you if I must."

Taking a deep breath and moving slowly, Longarm pulled himself up on the long, sloping muddy bank.

He looked around, stunned with disbelief. A fragrant, fruitful green basin lay enclosed in a high wall of sandstone, which seemed to mark the end of this grand world, and to stand as a fortification against intrusion by outsiders. He felt himself a puny fragment, dwarfed by colossal growth and rich verdure, land softened and tamed and enriched by sweet and almost inconceivable persistence.

This plateau had once been a ridged and scarred waste, lying inside these slate faults, and sloping downward to the river. The jagged ranges loomed on all sides, enclosing it and concealing it within a circle of a thousand ragged peaks. Through it cut the Colorado, just now in full-crested majesty, but often looking like liquid mud. He could hardly believe the marvelous achievement in this lost vale. The violet-hued canyons lay clear to the north, and the naked bones of the slate and sandstone faults still showed the true nature of this blazing desert. But these people had embraced and utilized its awful barrenness, bringing life where there had been only death and awesome depths of unbroken silence.

He moved his gaze across the precise green rows of corn, the dark spread of vegetables, the shadowed area of the groves, the grasslands where cattle grazed, and above them, sheep in the rocky mesas. He thought he saw dark roofs, and then to the southwest he glimpsed a faint column of smoke against the rose-tinted sky.

"This place is on no maps I ever saw," he said aloud. He shook his head again. Birds sang or screeched in groves of willow and cottonwood. Distantly, cattle lowed. It was as if he had blundered into Eden.

"Don't make me kill you, stranger."

"You don't have to kill me. I'm no threat to you, or to your people."

"If we let you go, others will come," the voice persisted.

"Mister, you do hate hard."

Longarm squinted against the blaze of sunlight and stared upslope. At the rim of the rise stood a gaunt, weatherbeaten, and bearded man, holding his rifle fixed on Longarm. The man looked to be about fifty years old, though it was difficult to gauge accurately the ages of the bearded Mormons. They all looked as if they'd been born sixty-two years old.

This rifle-toting farmer wore a denim jacket over a butternut homemade shirt, and his jaw was heavily bearded. His nose protruded in a Roman hook descending from bushy brows and deep-set eyes to beard-shrouded mouth. Somehow he most resembled a bad photograph of Abe Lincoln, with wrinkled, morose, coffee-brown face. His homemade, wide-brimmed black hat shaded his eyes. His body, in much-washed denim overalls, was rail-thin. His oversized, bony hands gripped the rifle fiercely, and yet reluctantly. But not even the gun troubled Longarm as much as the farmer's eyes, shadowed under the brim of his felt hat; they were a fanatic's eyes.

Longarm stood up deliberately, taking his time and keeping his hands well out at his sides. Standing, he had to quickly set his long legs wide apart to keep from pitching forward on his face. The world spun about his head, and when his gaze focused again, he saw a young woman, slender and sedate in homespun dress and sunbonnet. She was not pretty, and there was not a touch of color in her dress or face or eyes. Even her hair, under the hood of her bonnet, seemed drab and mousy.

She stood well behind the armed farmer, past the line of the slope, in a dense patch of green underbrush. She did not move and she did not take her unyielding gaze from Longarm's face.

"Why did you come here to this place?" she said at last.

The farmer jerked his head around and said, "That will be enough from you, Chastity. You will not soil yourself looking on evil Gentiles." Then he whipped his gaze back and stood waiting, taut, for Longarm's answer.

"I didn't come from choice," Longarm said. "I swear I have no evil intentions toward you, your people, or your lands. Put that gun away and let's talk this over."

The farmer hesitated. Clearly, murder was the last thing he wanted on his conscience, even in defense of his home. For a moment it looked as if he might lower the rifle, but then he changed his mind.

He shook his head, holding the rifle fixed on Longarm's belt buckle. "Come up the slope," he said at last. "I shall let the Elders decide your fate."

"That's damned decent of you," Longarm said.

Both the bearded man and young Chastity gasped in horrified unison. The farmer said, voice rasping, "We don't need your ugly blasphemy in this place. Swearing is a mortal sin in God's eyes, and we will not tolerate it."

Longarm nodded. "It's your home," he said. "You make the rules and I'll live by 'em." He laid hard stress on the word *live*.

There was no response from the farmer or the woman.

Longarm drew a deep breath and took a long step up the slope. His legs trembled like a newborn calf's, and he stumbled and almost fell, but managed to catch himself.

"Have you been drinking hard liquor?" the farmer demanded, the gun straightening in his grip.

"Look, I've been in the water—in that river—all day and all night."

The farmer's bearded face darkened. His head tilted and his fanatic eyes glittered. "Do not add lying to your other sins. Lying is an abomination before God."

It occurred to Longarm that the Mormon God was even more wrathful than the vengeful God of the Old Testament, and didn't allow much leeway for human frailty. No wonder the Mormons worked so hard in their fields; God's rules left them damned little else to do. But he decided not to give voice to his thoughts; diplomacy seemed the better part of valor at this moment. He said in a reasonable tone, though the world wheeled and skidded before him, the sun blazed blindingly, and the birds were shrill and penetrating inside his skull, "I'm not lying. Do you know where Carp is?"

The farmer shook his head. He glanced at Chastity, who shrugged. "No."

"How about Las Vegas?"

"I've heard of Las Vegas. I have never been there."

"Nor I," said Chastity.

"Nor had any wish to go," the bearded one said in a harsh tone meant to reprove the girl.

"Nor had any wish to," she added as if it were part of a memorized litany.

Longarm sighed; the world settled slightly, his legs no longer trembled. "You folks don't get around a lot, do you?"

"We've no need—no wish—to leave this valley," the man said.

Chastity nodded, but she seemed less positive than the rifle-toting farmer.

"How long have you lived here—in Alamut?" Longarm asked, faintly troubled by that unfamiliar name, though he could not say why.

"I have lived here all my life," the man said. "This valley is farmed by second-generation Mormons. We live in peace here with the Havasu Indians. That is the way we want it."

"I was born here too," Chastity said.

"Do you stay in Alamut because you want to?" Longarm asked. "Or because your father wants you to?"

The saddle-brown face went ashen beneath the salty beard. The man's hands trembled on his rifle. "Chastity is not my daughter," he said, voice quavering. "I am Elder Abel McFee and Chastity is my wife—my youngest wife."

"Congratulations," Longarm said.

Elder McFee and his newest wife herded Longarm up from the river and across the fertile farmland, deep with vegetables and sharp with the tangy, rich odors of growing things.

By the time they entered the town limits, people were coming in from fields, barns, outhouses, and grazelands. The men marched boldly, talking to each other, excited and outraged. The women were quieter, moving in silent knots, but watching everything with intense curiosity.

When they got to the jail, a considerable crowd had gathered in front of the building. The lockup was an adobe building that squatted alone in a grassy square, shaded by a single cottonwood tree.

Longarm glanced around, astonished. Though he was convinced that Alamut was not even shown on Billy Vail's huge map of Nevada, the town was well laid out, substantial, with a look of age about it. He got the strange feeling that the parents and grandparents of these disciples had lost themselves in this vast "open federal land." They had forgotten the outside world, and had been forgotten by it.

At the small, square, adobe edifice of the town jail, McFee ordered Longarm to stop. "We'll just wait for Law Officer Russell Battles," the Elder said.

"Is this Battles your sheriff?" Longarm said

"Elder Battles is an officer of the Lord, and an official of our true God. He answers only to Elder Noah Waymeyer himself." McFee nodded bleakly. "He will know what to do about you."

"What you got there, Abel?" a bearded man asked.

"Where'd you find him?" said another.

"Tryin' to rustle our cattle?"

"Stealin', anyhow. That's for sure. You can look at him and see he be a Gentile. A thievin' Gentile."

"We'll just hold him for Officer Battles," McFee said. "He may be the dog you say he is. But let us not be hasty, or act rashly. Officer Battles will know what is best."

"You catch him thievin', Abel?"

Abel shook his head. He seemed about not to speak at all, then something resembling a crooked smile twisted the corners of his mouth.

"Not exactly," the rail-thin man said, and the way he spoke caused a faint ripple of laughter to course through the crowd of men. Even the women glanced at each other, though none of them actually smiled.

Longarm sighed. Despite appearances, it looked as if Elder Abel McFee was the comedian of the town, who kept everybody feeling good and almost laughing out loud.

"What were he doin', Abel?" somebody prompted.

"Tell us, Abel. Tell us. What were he doing?"

"He was lying like a sick dog on the bank of the river,"

McFee said. "And my wife and I stared at him for a long time, thinking him dead. He didn't move a muscle until I put a rifle bullet within inches of his face."

"Thought I heard gunfire," somebody said, nodding.

"That's what you heard," Abel McFee said. "Then he tells us he's been floating two days or so in the river."

The spectators almost laughed aloud. They did look at each other, grimacing behind their beards and shaking their heads. "An abomination before God," an aging man said.

"My very words," Abel McFee agreed. "When he wouldn't tell us the truth and made no offer to show us where his boat was hid, I brought him up here. If he's to be executed, I wanted the town to do it. I don't care to have even the blood of a Gentile on my hands."

"Abel McFee always was a gentle man," somebody said.

Another Elder nodded seriously, agreeing. "I swear, I believe Abel wouldn't kill game or animals—except for food."

"I just didn't want his blood on my hands," Abel said.

A huge, bearded man wearing bib overalls, stretched taut over a massive potbelly, pushed his way through the ring of onlookers. Longarm knew this would be the high sheriff, or whatever name the Mormons gave their peace officer, even before anyone spoke his name. He looked young despite his grizzled, shaggy face, and his brown eyes were set close together, youthful, yet steely hard and brutal.

"Where did this Gentile come from?" Battles asked.

Somebody in the crowd laughed. "From the river, Elder Battles. From swimming two days in the Colorado."

Some of the men had to hold back their amusement, but Battles was not in the least amused. He stared into Longarm's face. He was only an inch or so shorter in his thick-heeled boots.

"Who are you?" Battles said.

"I'm Custis Long, a deputy U.S. marshal."

"A deputy U.S. marshal, eh?" Battles said. "You look like a hobo to me. A thievin' Gentile tramp. What were you trying to steal?"

"He was asleep when I found him, Elder Battles," McFee said.

"Asleep? Where?"

"On the bank of the river," Longarm answered. "I got washed up there when the flash flood let up a little during the night. I got caught in the flood up around Carp yesterday morning, and—"

"Carp? Carp!" Battles clenched his fists at his sides. He looked as if he had been pushed beyond human endurance. "Are you asking reasonable folk to believe you survived a flash flood—and stayed in that river more than eighty miles? And through canyon rapids?"

Longarm exhaled heavily, but said nothing.

"There's no sense lying, Long, or whatever your name is. We'll get the truth out of you," Battles said. "If you're a deputy U.S. marshal, maybe you can show us your badge?"

"I lost it," Longarm said.

"And your identification. I reckon you lost that too?"

Longarm spread his hands. "As hard as it is for you to believe, I did have a badge, and I did have identification. Up in Carp."

Battles chewed hard on his underlip. "You'll do well to put Carp out of your mind, and out of your lying mouth. Nobody believes you came from Carp. Any more than we believe you are a U.S. marshal—"

"Deputy marshal. You could send a telegraph to Chief Marshal Vail in Denver—"

"We have no telegraph in this valley," Battles said.

"An instrument of the devil," somebody said.

Battles unlocked the door of the jail and jerked it open. The barred entrance was double-width, wide enough almost to accommodate a small cart and donkey. His huge hand, white-knuckled, gripped the bars.

"All right, Long—or whatever your name is." Russell Battles gestured with his head toward the inside of the cell. "Inside."

"There's no sense in this," Longarm said, exasperated. "Give me a chance. I can prove—"

"Oh, we're going to give you a chance, Gentile," Battles said. "We're going to give you a chance to appear before Elder Noah Waymeyer, as soon as the Elder has the time to see you."

"Who is Elder Waymeyer?"

"He is our spiritual leader," one of the older men said. "He came unto us from the great Tabernacle at Salt Lake City itself. We accept the word of Elder Waymeyer as we take the preachings of the sainted Brother Smith or Brigham Young—or even God Jehovah himself."

"Sounds like quite a man."

Battles suddenly snagged Longarm's arm and half hurled him into the cell. "We don't need your heathen disrespect. You'd best think with kind thoughts on Elder Noah Waymeyer, because, friend, I can tell you one thing—your life depends on the glorious decision of Elder Waymeyer himself."

The cell doors of the jail slammed shut and Elder Battles locked the door. But the crowd outside did not disperse. They remained standing in the sun, staring at Longarm as if they'd never seen his like before, as if he were a freak in a sideshow.

Ignoring the crowd, Longarm prowled the cubicle as a caged panther might walk its cell. The place was dim with shadows and sparsely furnished. There was an iron cot with no mattress, but a blanket was folded neatly at its foot. In the corner was an earthenware slops jar. The flooring was rough adobe, as were the walls.

Battles stood at the bars. "No sense looking for a way out, Gentile. This here is an escape-proof jail. It's sixty years old and nobody has never broke out of it yet."

"Spend your time praying," a gray-bearded elder advised. "Your one hope of getting out of here lies in the compassion of Elder Waymeyer."

Longarm strode to the bars. "Do I pray directly to Elder Waymeyer, or do I have to go through God?"

The people gasped at his blasphemy and retreated from the bars.

Longarm walked across the room to a shaft of sunlight allowed into the gloom by a high, recessed, and barred window. He sagged down in the saffron warmth and hugged his knees.

He was aware of the huge-shouldered Elder Battles stalking away. He shrugged. He was glad to see him go. He only wished the other curious, suspicious people would disappear. But most of them remained in the sunlight, gazing in at him raptly.

He grinned at them. "Want to thank you for the nice comfortable quarters, folks," he said. "I think I'm going to be mighty satisfied here."

They peered silently through the bars at him. Not only was he a prisoner and a stranger, he was a Gentile. Some of them had never seen a real, live Gentile before. They stood gaping outside the bars, studying him and trying to reconcile in their own minds what he looked like, and what they had been told a heathen Gentile from the outside would be.

"How am I going to get a chance to escape, if you people stand there watching me?" he asked.

One of the older men took this in desperate seriousness. "Oh, you can't escape, heathen. There is no hope for that."

"Oh?" Longarm shook his head. "I got some news for you, Elder. 'Escape-proof' is just a belief in somebody's mind. A jail is escape-proof to them that believe it is. To him that don't believe it, why, it's just another room in another building."

They stood a moment, scarcely breathing, digesting this. They gazed at each other, and then ten or twelve of them suddenly heeled around and hurried away across the compound. The others retreated across the hard-packed street, to where the women stood.

An aging man ran close to the barred door. He stood staring in. At last he blurted out, "You'll never break out of this cell." Then he turned and ran back across the street.

Longarm pursued him as far as the barred door. He yelled, "You a betting man, Elder?"

"Gambling is forbidden," a woman cried out.

Longarm grinned and nodded. "I know, Mother. An abomination before God."

The crowd thinned gradually. Longarm returned to his sunny square in the gloomy cell and hunkered there, staring at the floor. The sun rose, heating the room almost unbearably.

When he glanced out at the street, most of the spectators had gone off to their chores, or their noon meal.

Food. His stomach growled.

He exhaled heavily. He couldn't really think about food, even after these long hours. He was hungry, but mostly his hunger was for identity, for proof that he was who he said he was, for some way to get word to Billy Vail in Denver, for the right to get out of this place, to escape this valley forever. It looked like an Eden in the desert, but already, after only a few hours, he knew better.

He walked from the door to the dark wall and back again. He was in a hell of a spot, any way he looked at it. He had not a cent of money, no weapons, no wallet, no badge, no scrap of identification. Little Billy Bates had done his job well; the sun-dried road agent was a true professional, a craftsman at his art. He had wanted to leave no trace of identification on Longarm, and he had accomplished that, in spades.

He gripped the bars, staring out across the silent compound, the groves, the gardens, the silent houses, the buff sandstone cliffs beyond. What had happened to him was what he would have sworn could never happen. He was abandoned and lost and alone, a nameless stranger in a hostile land . . .

Someone unlocked the barred door, and Longarm looked up.

He had never seen the bearded man before, but he recognized the rifle as a Henry, cocked and ready in the crook of his arm.

The fellow opened the door only enough to permit Chastity McFee to enter. She carried a pot of coffee and a couple of steaming, covered dishes.

"I brought your lunch," she said.

He smiled. "That growling you hear is my stomach trying to thank you, Chastity."

She nodded and set the tray of food on the floor near him. The aroma of coffee, the scent of food attacked him, and he felt lightheaded for a moment.

He grinned at Chastity, and the startled young woman said, "What in the world have you got to smile about?"

"That you're such a good cook."

She bit her lip. "I didn't cook it. The Elder's first wife does all the cooking. But she is very good. Her name is Esmeralda. She is even older than Elder McFee. They have been married a very long time."

He poured coffee into a tin cup and drank it. The scalding liquid was like nectar. He smacked his lips. He gazed at Chastity over the rim of the cup. "I'll bet Elder Abel McFee was happy to get you."

She blushed. "I'll come back and get the tray when you have finished your dinner."

"All right." He nodded and then said, "Chastity?"

She paused and glanced over her shoulder. Her face was pale and rigid. "Yes?"

"I wonder if you would do something for me?" he said.

Her face got grayer. She shook her head, looking frightened. "Oh, I could never help you escape. I could not. You must not even ask me."

"It's not that," he said, chewing on a thick slab of hot bread spread with fresh butter. "Oh, it's not that at all. Oh, no. You see, escaping this place is a matter of honor. I must do that alone."

She gasped. "Oh, please," she said. "Don't try that. They will kill you. Even if you did escape this cell, they would kill you. You could never get away alive."

He stared at her. "You know, don't you, Chastity? You know because you've tried."

She gasped again and shook her head, confused and disturbed. "I must go. You must not talk like that. You must never say things like that." She hesitated, then went on, "Please do not try to escape. Both Elder Abel and I believe there is every possibility that if you are sentenced at all, it will be a very light sentence."

"I keep remembering that your husband told me he could never let me leave this valley alive. I heard them call him a gentle man. What chance do I have with the others?"

"You must be patient," she whispered. "I promise you this. Both the Elder and I will speak for you at your trial."

"Why would you do that?"

She bit her lip. "Because now we think we were wrong."

He chewed on a piece of beef from a stew rich with hunks of potatoes and carrots. "Now, when it's too late, you believe I did float into this paradise on a log, eh?"

"I don't know," she said. "I don't know what I believe. I must go."

"If you were to testify for me, you and your husband, that would be going against the will of the Disciples. You could get in trouble."

"I don't know." She shook her head again. "You get me all mixed up. You must let me alone. I must go."

"Go with God," he said.

She winced and hurried to the barred door. There she paused. "What was it you wanted me to do for you?"

"A cigar, Chastity," he said. "I'd give my right arm for a good smoke."

She shook her head. "You know I can't do that. There is no way. There are no cigars allowed in the valley. You know in your heart that tobacco is an instrument of the devil and forbidden by the True Church."

"Oh, yes. That's right. Another abomination before God." He grinned at her. "You've got so many abominations, Chastity, I don't see how you keep track of them."

She stepped through the narrow opening and slammed the door behind her. She gazed at him through the bars. "I want to say only that I am sorry. Both Elder McFee and I—we wish there were something we could do to help you."

He waved at her casually and shook his head. "I wish there was too, Chastity."

Chapter 5

With his wrists secured in handcuffs before him, Longarm was led into the Alamut meeting house.

This building, which served for church services, town meetings, trials, or any other entertainments permitted by the Latter-Day Saints' canons, was as austere as the town jail, though slightly larger. The walls were bare of pictures, paintings, statuary, or icons of any kind. The pinewood benches were rough and sturdily made, with thick slab backrests, and never meant for comfort. He supposed life on this earth was never intended for the bodily comfort of these people.

At the front of the room was a pinewood table, its top at least rubbed and polished, with nine chairs set along it facing the benches, for the presiding Elders.

The room was crowded, every space on the rough pine benches occupied. An expectant chatter buzzed across the somber-faced audience. All wore dark clothing without a hint of color. The women sat in silence, heads lowered humbly.

When Longarm was led in, even the women raised their eyes enough to stare at this stranger from the outside. Clearly they had never seen anything quite like him, or expected to in this serene and verdant valley.

He glanced at them and found not a friendly face, or even a disinterested one. The hatred that human beings reserve for anything they don't know glittered in all the eyes fixed on him, tautened every mouth, stretched every nerve, loosed every prejudice.

Longarm was led to a wooden chair between the polished table and the first row of onlookers. The chair was placed so it faced the far side wall, so that Longarm's profile was to both audience and judges. He sat with his manacled hands in his lap and stared through the window opposite him at birds scolding in the lower branches of a cottonwood tree. Beyond lay the quiet fields, vividly green against the tan sand of the arid plains inside the ring of sandstone cliffs.

Seven of the presiding Elders entered the spartan room and seated themselves rigidly and silently at the table, leaving the center chair unoccupied. A guilty stillness settled over the room, and people stirred, preparing for the trial. Deerflies buzzed at the open windows; distantly, a jackass brayed and cattle lowed, but somehow all sounds only intensified the silence.

At last Elder Noah Waymeyer entered the room.

Longarm recognized the leader of the community, even though he had never seen him before.

The Mormons waited respectfully for Waymeyer to take his place at the head table.

Waymeyer moved deliberately, unhurriedly. His gaze seemed turned inward, as though he actually saw neither the tethered prisoner nor the townspeople on their benches. One might almost have believed the Elder was in communication with some higher tribunal, preoccupied and intent.

The first thing Longarm noticed about Elder Noah Waymeyer was that the man was bigger than all the other Elders, almost as if he had succeeded to leadership on physical size alone.

Longarm admitted that of course this was hardly likely to be true. It was just that in his profession of pursuing and confronting felons, physical size and strength were always a first consideration. And Waymeyer looked as if he *could* have wrested anything he wanted from these people on the basis of physical superiority alone.

The second thing Longarm noticed was shocking. Elder Waymeyer was a young man—if anything, no more than a year or so older than Longarm himself. There was youthfulness in his face, his thick beard, his hooded eyes, the dexterity of his arms, the very way he moved. And the advanced age of most of the other Elders pointed up Noah Waymeyer's comparative youthfulness.

Beside him, the gray-haired elders waited, deeply respectful, awed, almost fearful.

Next, Longarm's scrutiny found another oddity about the spiritual leader of Alamut. Noah Waymeyer was the only man in the valley who wore store-bought clothing. His trousers, boots, shirt, and hat all had been bought outside the walls of this lost basin. Waymeyer demonstrated his superiority to the ordinary flock in more ways than one.

Waymeyer's shoulders were as broad as Longarm's and far beefier. His biceps and chest muscles strained against the fabric of his clothing. His scarred fists were like hams, and he kept clenching them on the top of the table, almost involuntarily.

Waymeyer's eyes at last contemplated Longarm from under bushy, shapeless brows. Longarm winced faintly. Elder Waymeyer's eyes were the most fearful of all these fanatics'—they were dead gray, empty, cold.

Like his arms and shoulders, Waymeyer's jowls were heavy, his cheeks puffy. He was bull-necked, and had loosened the top button of his shirt as if his collar chafed him. He bent his head and spat into a brass spittoon placed beside his chair. Longarm saw that Elder Waymeyer was the only man in the room afforded this convenience, too.

As Longarm watched the Elder, he was troubled by a gnawing sense of wrong. He forced himself to admit he was prejudiced against the presiding judge, as any felon likely despises the judiciary on sight. He tried in vain to find something positive in his scrutiny of the spiritual leader of Alamut.

Elder Noah Waymeyer behaved decorously; he appeared devout, a truly holy man. Maybe, after all, this was all that was important to his followers.

For a long moment those dead gray eyes fixed themselves on Longarm with a strange, unrelenting ferocity. Then the Elder smiled in faint, sad way. "We are ready to begin," he said in a low voice.

From the first row of benches, Peace Officer Russell Battles stood up. He said, "We are gathered, Brother Noah, to hear the charges—and your holy judgment—against this heathen.

61

He is a nameless Gentile, without identification, who came into this valley on the river." He told how Elder Abel McFee and his wife Chastity had discovered the stranger on the riverbank. "This man will not tell us why he is here."

Longarm said, "I've tried to tell you."

The Elder's gray eyes fastened themselves for a moment on the peace official, with that faint, sad, and querulous smile. "Is this true, Brother Russell?"

Battles's bearded mouth twisted with contempt. "He has told us many lies. But he has proved only that he lies, that he cannot be trusted. He has declared many things that he cannot prove. We believe he has come among us as a thief or a spy."

Waymeyer merely smiled in that sad, patient way. "Our trial will determine why the Gentile came among us."

Battles nodded respectfully. "That is why we have come before you, Brother Noah."

Waymeyer sat for some moments, his fists clenched on the polished tabletop, staring at Longarm. The elders beside Waymeyer shifted in their chairs. Several people on the benches cleared their throats in the stillness, but nobody moved. At last the leader inquired in a soft, yet inflexible tone, "Where did you first hear of Alamut?"

"I never did hear of it," Longarm said. "I never saw it on any map. It is a strange name for a Mormon town, isn't it?"

"We'll ask the questions," Waymeyer reminded him. "Like the name Zion or New Zion, Alamut is the name of our Latter-Day Saints' community."

"Only I've heard of Zion before."

The voice remained soft, steellike. "You are on trial here; we are not. I ask you now: Are you fleeing from the law of the United States?"

"I am not a fugitive from the law." Longarm grinned coldly. "I am not now. I never have been."

"You are not running away from outside justice?"

"I am a law officer of the United States. I am a federal deputy marshal."

Noah Waymeyer almost smiled, but it was a smile of contempt. "Can you prove this?"

Longarm drew a deep breath. "Yes I can."

"Will you produce that proof, please?"

"I can do that only by getting word to the office of the chief marshal in Denver."

Waymeyer shook his shaggy head. "I am afraid that would not be acceptable. It would require a month at least to send and receive such information."

"You could send a letter to Las Vegas. How far is that?"

"No more than twenty miles. But it is twenty miles of wild ranges and open desert. Again, I remind you, we will ask the questions."

"A letter sent to Las Vegas could be put on the eastbound limited. It could be in Denver overnight."

"However," the patient voice pointed out, "wagons go from Alamut through the narrow pass to Las Vegas only once a month. A matter of four days. Two days each way. The wagon train just returned this week."

"And so it will be a month before you'll send another?"

"That's right," Waymeyer replied, almost lazily.

Longarm spoke sharply. "Can't you send a rider?"

"A rider, eh?" Waymeyer appeared to ponder this. "Perhaps we could." He shook his head. "But I don't believe we need to do that."

The rustling and nodding of the crowd told Longarm that Waymeyer's people supported their leader wholeheartedly.

There would be no rider.

"Why did you come here?" Waymeyer asked after a brief, taut silence.

"I've told your people. They don't believe me."

"We have had other criminals in the past. Perhaps we have learned what we can and cannot believe from heathen lips."

Longarm stared back at the leader. "What are you charging me with?"

Again the Elder gave him a sadly patient smile, without any trace of compassion in it. Longarm felt his nerves hitch tighter in the pit of his belly. The outcome of this trial was already determined. This was all window dressing. It was also like a cat playing with a mouse.

"As I explained to you before," Elder Waymeyer said, "we will ask the questions. I hope I don't have to keep reminding you—you are here, before these good people, not because you have any rights before a bar of justice, but because you intruded upon their lands, forced your way into their home. You are here at their sufferance."

"Are you saying this is not a part of the United States?" Longarm demanded.

"It is *our* part of the United States," Waymeyer replied. Again there was a loud murmur of agreement and a nodding of heads. "Do not fear, Gentile. You will be afforded greater justice from this gathering than *they* ever received at the hands of your people and your government."

"I remind you, it is your government too," Longarm said.

"And yet, I believe you will agree, it is a long way from Alamut." Waymeyer spat again.

Longarm asked again, "What are you charging me with?"

"Why don't you let us ask the questions?" Waymeyer inquired. "We could proceed so much more neatly and quickly. I can say this, at this time, and with no further inquiry—we can, if nothing else, charge you with vagrancy. Alamut has a very strictly enforced vagrancy law. If you have not yet committed any other crime against us, you have broken our vagrancy law by coming into our valley uninvited—"

"And unintentionally."

"You have no identification, no visible means of support."

"I've tried to tell you people. I am a lawman. I was attacked, assaulted, thrown into—"

The people stamped their feet, the men's boots resounding against the flooring. They shouted until Longarm's voice could no longer even be heard in the din.

Shouted down, Longarm fell silent. Waymeyer raised his thick arm, silencing the crowd. His voice was not as soft as before. The steel glinted in it. He had demonstrated that he was a patient man whose patience was being sorely tested. He rubbed his throat and spat again into the spittoon. "Will you let us continue now?"

When Longarm shrugged, Waymeyer continued, "Any river-running scamp can *say* he is a deputy U.S. marshal. Would you agree with that? Of course you would. You *say* you are a federal marshal. Where is your proof?"

The crowd rustled. Longarm was surprised they didn't leap to their feet to demonstrate against him and for their spiritual leader.

Exasperated, Longarm glared back at the man across the polished table. "All right," he said. "I confess. I came here uninvited. But I am willing now to right that error."

"Are you? In what way?"

"You have my offer. You people follow me back down to the riverbank. I'll jump into the river and be on my way."

The crowd muttered angrily, and Noah Waymeyer shook his head. "That's enough, Gentile! You shall not be permitted to make a mockery of this court."

"You're doing that without any help from me, old son," Longarm replied in a cold, dead voice precisely matching Waymeyer's.

Waymeyer conferred for some moments with the Elders closest on each side of him. The room remained silent. When he resumed questioning, his voice was harder, with little patience remaining in it.

"I warn you, heathen. You shall not be permitted to rouse us to rashness. We shall show the same fortitude, patience, and strength we showed through the cruel persecutions of your people against ours, through the long exodus and exile, the same patience enabled us to outlast and defeat you despised Gentiles."

The Elders in the room spoke aloud, a guttural mutter of approval. Longarm stared at Waymeyer. He disagreed with everything the man said, but there was one thing he could not doubt, and this was the man's sincerity. These people blindly followed everything they were told, every word their leader spoke, as if it were Holy Writ.

"I ask you now, Gentile," Waymeyer said, his voice hard, "where is your boat hidden?"

"I have no boat."

"Do you believe we will not find it?"

"I have no boat."

"Did you come into this valley alone?"

Longarm nodded. "On a log."

The crowd muttered angrily at this, but Waymeyer lifted his hand for silence, then said, "How many confederates came with you?"

"I came here alone."

"Where are they waiting?"

"Who?"

"Your confederates. Where do they hide, waiting to strike us in the night?"

Longarm was almost ready to laugh aloud, but he could not laugh through the rage that welled up in him. He said, voice low and tense, "You are the most suspicious, mistrustful human beings I've ever met."

"Why should we trust you?"

Longarm shrugged. "Because I came here by mistake. Because I have no evil intentions toward any of you. Because I am willing to leave anytime you will let me."

"You'd like us to believe that, wouldn't you?"

"Sure."

Waymeyer straightened in his chair. His voice thundered in the stillness of the bare room. "Are you a Gentile?"

"I guess so. I'm not a Latter-Day Saint."

"Do you admit that the Gentiles have persecuted the Chosen People?"

"I've heard of cruelty and persecution—"

"Even ambush and murder?"

"Even that. The record of our country—and yours—is not too clean in its treatment of any minorities—black, red, Mormon, or otherwise."

"Do you admit to this persecution?"

"My folks raised me up to treat everybody fair, and not to hurt or speak ill of any man—or woman—unless they tried to hurt or slander somebody else."

Waymeyer stared at him with those ash-dead eyes, as if Longarm were beneath his contempt, past even his great understanding. He said, "And you confess to this court that you feel no qualms of conscience?"

"About what happened to the Mormons? No. They had a tough time. But I ain't persecuted anybody. I am well received by the Elders and the Church in Salt Lake City. I returned a Mormon woman once who had been kidnapped by a bunch who called themselves the Avenging Angels. I have worked with the Mormons and they have worked with me."

Waymeyer's bearded mouth twisted, and his eyes gleamed between cold hatred and even colder pity. "I suppose you can prove that too?"

Longarm shrugged his shoulders. "Not at this moment."

"Where is your boat hidden?"

"My God!"

"When did you accept Christ?"

"Don't quite know what you mean. I respect any man who believes something so much he's willing to die for it."

"Have you been born again?"

"Not recently." Then Longarm paused, remembering the rushing river, the log, and the rapids. "I don't know. Maybe I have."

66

"Are you an Antichrist?"

"I'm a deputy U.S. marshal."

"When did you first deny Christ?"

"I took an oath to uphold and defend the U.S. Constitution when I was hired as a deputy marshal. That's about it."

"Why have men like you sworn in their hearts to destroy our people?"

"I don't know. You'd have to ask them."

"I am asking *you*. Why have you come here to destroy us?"

"Hell, it was a dull week. I figured, why not?"

"Your blasphemy will buy you little sympathy in this court, Gentile."

"I ain't been exactly overwhelmed by your compassion up to this moment, Brother."

"Do you insist that you came alone here to destroy us?"

"I came alone."

"Are there others with you?"

"I've lost track."

"Where are they?"

"Who?"

"Your hidden confederates. You will do well to confess. We shall have the truth from you."

"I doubt that."

"Do you?" Waymeyer said. "Why?"

"Because the truth is the last thing you want, Brother."

"How many are there?"

"There's just me and a log. Even the log's gone. Lucky for the log, I reckon."

"Why have you come here?"

"Would you believe me if I told you?"

"Where is your boat hidden?"

Elder Noah Waymeyer leaned back in his chair. A look of extreme pity creased his swollen face. When he stood up, all the others came hastily to their feet too.

Waymeyer gestured with his arms for the people to be seated. There was a rustling of clothing as they returned to the hard benches. The Elder went on standing. He said, "We come to that moment of great justice and right, common to every trial conducted in this community. We are now ready to hear words of defense spoken for the outsider." He moved his gaze across the crowded room. "Is there among us any to speak for the intruder?"

Silence greeted the question.

As Waymeyer exhaled heavily and moved to sit down, Elder Abel McFee suddenly stood. His young wife, Chastity, got up and went silently to stand beside him.

Gasps of shock and outrage whipped across the room. This had never happened before, even in the memory of the eldest member of the community. They had never expected to live to see it. Speaking for a defendant in Alamut was tantamount to heresy, blasphemy, and drinking alcoholic beverages.

Elder Waymeyer managed to control his outrage, shock, and dismay. He leaned upon both his clenched fists on the polished table and stared at the thin McFee and his youthful wife.

His voice shaking with disbelief, Waymeyer said, "Abel, what is the meaning of this?"

"It is something I must do, Brother," Abel McFee managed to say.

"And I," Chastity whispered almost inaudibly.

"And what is that, Brother Abel?" Elder Waymeyer inquired in a cold, dead tone.

"I must speak, Elder—in behalf of the stranger."

Waymeyer looked as if he might expire from shock and suppressed outrage, but he managed to nod. "What is it you wish you say?"

Abel McFee stared straight ahead. He spoke in a firm, yet quavering voice. He was frightened, but determined. Longarm watched him compassionately. "I did find the stranger. As he himself says. Alone. He was lying alone—and soaked—beside the river."

"But he was within our valley?" Waymeyer prodded.

"He was asleep," Chastity said in a firm, clear voice. "He was lying, wet and asleep, on the bank of the river."

Abel nodded. He continued to stare into the middle distance. "He slept. There was no sign of gun nor boat nor friends. It looked to be much as he says."

Voices raged from the benches in protest. Elder Waymeyer permitted this outcry to continue for some minutes, and then he waved his arms, asking mutely for silence.

"We are forced to say these things," Abel said.

"Who forces you, Brother?" Waymeyer inquired compassionately.

"Our belief in God," Abel replied. "Our belief that God would want us to speak the truth as we see it."

"And what truth is that?"

Abel sighed. "That it seems to us much as the stranger says. He did come alone and unarmed among us, not by design, but by some freakish accident."

"You cannot prove any of this, can you, Brother?" Elder Waymeyer asked.

Abel winced and shook his head. "Heresy!" the people shouted. "He has turned against us. Against his own people."

"That's not true," Abel said, shaking his head. His eyes brimmed with tears. "We must not lie—any of us."

"Do you say we lie?" a man demanded from among the spectators. "Do you say the Elders of our Church lie?"

Noah Waymeyer lifted his arms, pleading for silence. He went around the table and stood beside Abel McFee and Chastity. Somehow, with the sun shining on them through the open window, they reminded Longarm forcefully of a Sunday school print of Jesus Christ with two lost sheep.

Waymeyer's dead eyes looked sad and disturbed. He lifted his arms and shook his head again. "Please," he said, addressing the crowded room, "let us not turn against our own. Let us not condemn the good Elder McFee and his wife. Not without patient consideration of all conditions."

"You are a great and gentle man, Elder Waymeyer," a woman said.

"Your compassion is as great as life," a man said.

"Your understanding surpasseth understanding," said an Elder at the table.

Elder Waymeyer bowed his head humbly, accepting their accolades as nothing more than his due. When he spoke, his voice dripped compassion. "I believe I can explain what has happened here. I can see in my heart—and I pray I can make you people understand, who have known Abel for a good and faithful neighbor all these years—what has happened to Brother Abel and Sister Chastity."

"Speak, Brother!"

"Tell us, Elder!"

"In God's name, Elder, help us understand these poor misguided souls!"

"Help us, Elder! Before God! Make us understand their heresy, their blasphemy!"

"We know that the laws of Alamut permit our people to shoot intruders who will not quickly and willingly depart our land. We have been told that Elder McFee's first decision was to shoot the intruder. Why? Because in his heart, Brother Abel *knew* the stranger to be a heathen, a Gentile, an enemy.

"But—they were alone on that bank with the Antichrist, with this heathen son of Satan, with the great power of Satan to befuddle and bewitch good people. That is what has happened to Abel and Chastity. The heathen has bewitched them."

Abel McFee and all of his wives were removed from the courtroom and the trial was allowed to proceed. Waymeyer asked if there were others to speak for the prisoner, but of course there were none.

Elder Waymeyer sat for a long time at the table, his head in his hands, arms resting on his elbows. Cynically, Longarm found himself wondering whether the spiritual leader was contemplating Good and Evil, hiding his secret laughter from his gullible flock, or simply admiring himself in the gleaming surface.

At last Waymeyer looked up and gazed unblinkingly at Longarm. "The prisoner will stand," the Elder said at last.

When Longarm stood up, two men appeared suddenly, armed and sullen, to stand at each side of him.

Waymeyer stared at Longarm as if consumed with pity. "Have you anything to say before I pronounce sentence, Gentile?"

Longarm met his gaze. "Would it help me to speak?"

Waymeyer shook his head. "Not at all."

Longarm grinned coldly. "Then I have nothing to say."

Waymeyer exhaled and nodded. When he spoke, his voice was unctuous. "You are wise, prisoner, not to add lying and blasphemy to your crimes against my people."

Longarm smiled. "Oh, I'm wiser than hell after a day in your town, Elder."

"May your widsom increase under our tutelage," Waymeyer said, and Longarm would have sworn the big man had to hold back a savage smirk of self-satisfaction.

The room settled down, waiting tensely for the imposition of sentence upon the stranger.

"You have erred and sinned grievously against us," Waymeyer said. "You have intruded, unwelcome and unwanted, upon our lands. You have forced yourself upon us. You have disturbed and distressed the weaker ones among us.

"We do not know your motive for coming here. Too, we are not in a position to know what crimes you may have committed against law and order beyond the confines of our valley. For that reason we shall limit ourselves to imposing punishment to fit the one crime of which you are obviously guilty: vagrancy."

"Vagrancy?" The word burst from Longarm's mouth. "Is that what all this has been about? No court imposes anything but probation for simple vagrancy."

"That may be true in the godless world beyond our valley, prisoner. But our law is plainly stated and requires certain retribution. However, I believe you will find us lenient with you. Our compassion will be a lesson to your brothers on the outside, and to all bloodthirsty, heathen Gentiles.

"I find you guilty of vagrancy."

Longarm sighed heavily and waited. The Elder glanced at the men on both sides of him, but did not speak to them. He turned back and faced the prisoner. "The punishment for vagrancy in Alamut is clear. Fifty days in jail, or fifty dollars."

There was a general stirring, nodding, and whispering of assent in the audience. Elder Waymeyer hesitated, staring at Longarm.

"What do you expect me to say?" Longarm inquired.

"Which will it be, prisoner? Will you pay the fifty-dollar fine and go free?"

Longarm laughed at him. "Why, Brother, you know I don't have fifty *cents* on me."

Waymeyer's face darkened. "I know you are a vagrant. I can tell you, you will work your fine off. In our fields. In leg irons, to be certain you remain with us for the term of your sentence. You will be credited one dollar a day. And so you may expect to go free—and leave this valley—in fifty days."

The room was silent. Waymeyer stood unmoving, his face implacable, watching Longarm. Longarm met his gaze, looked at each of the Elders at the table, and then glanced at the sea of hostile faces in the somber room.

He shrugged and shook his head. "If you're waiting for me to thank you, Elder, you might as well go ahead and close this meeting."

Waymeyer's big fist slammed down on the polished table-top. Somehow, to Longarm, the sound was the slamming of those iron-barred doors at the town jail. The townspeople sat silently for a moment, then got up and began to file out of the meeting house.

The trial was over.

Chapter 6

Still handcuffed, Longarm was led by two armed men out of the Alamut town hall and across the main street of the village to the blacksmith's shop. The desert sun blazed above the valley, a blistering fireball.

He glanced at the Mormon settlement as he was shoved along by the two bully boys on each side of him. The town was self-contained: a tannery, leather shops, a general supply store, everything a people might need to sustain them in a remote place almost entirely cut off from the outside world.

Longarm slowed, and the fellow on his left drove his fist into his back in a sharp kidney punch. "Keep moving, Long. We'll tell you when to stop."

Longarm sucked in an agonized breath and looked at the heavyset man who had struck him. He was bearded like all the others, swarthy-faced, his eyes deadly slits in a fat face. He looked as if he lived well on this land. "What else do you bastards do in a place like this for excitement?"

The man on the other side of Longarm laughed. He was uglier even than his keg-chested partner, his beard shabby, his clothing soiled. "Don't worry about us, Long. A man can find plenty to excite him when he's the bodyguard for the Chief Apostle of the Church Council."

Longarm grinned coldly, glancing at the two bully boys. They seemed a year or so younger than Noah Waymeyer, but they lacked any tangible intelligence. The prisons and the owl-hoot trails were populated with characters like these two in the world outside this valley. He reckoned that even here in Alamut they might be imprisoned, except that they served Noah Waymeyer.

Longarm glanced toward the shabbier man and winked. "Reckon a big hombre like you sees any woman he wants, he can just take her, huh?"

The man on the other side of him struck Longarm again in the kidney. "Just shut up and keep moving," he said. "We'll tell you what you need to know."

Longarm kept walking, feeling the gazes of unseen villagers upon them. He glanced over his shoulder at the thick-chested man who'd struck him. "What's your name, partner?"

"Bales Cutlip. What's it to you?"

"Well, I just wanted to tell you, Bales. You better pray to your Mormon God that I don't ever get out of these handcuffs."

Bales Cutlip brayed with laughter. "You hear that, Gowdy? Some tough hombre, huh? Listen, Long, I'll worry about you when I have to. Meantime, I lose no sleep over it."

"I just thought it'd be only fair to tell you," Longarm said in a flat tone. "I keep score."

They were at the open entrance of the blacksmith shop now. Bales Cutlip struck Longarm in the kidney again, and then shoved him across the work area, almost to the anvil. "So do I, mister. Now shut your mouth and do what you're told— *when* you're told—and you'll be healthier."

"You don't want me too healthy, Bales," Longarm said.

Cutlip brayed again and called to the youthful blacksmith. "Got a rush job for you here, Haswell. Need ankle irons and chains for this prisoner. Fast. Got to get him out to the fields whilst there's plenty of sunlight." Cutlip roared at his own joke.

Haswell nodded, but said nothing. Gowdy said, "The Elder said to be sure that chain is measured right."

Again, the young blacksmith nodded, without bothering to speak. Tendons stretched and muscles rippled across his bare chest and arms. He looked as tough and massive as a buffalo, and yet about him—in his youthful face and eyes—there was almost a gentle look.

74

The shackles were clamped to Longarm's bare ankles. As Haswell completed this task and secured a length of chain between the ankle irons, Cutlip was casually draped over a stone table, cutting off the tops of Longarm's cavalry boots. Then, laughing, he tossed the bottom parts at Longarm's feet and told him to put them on. Longarm's face was cold. "I'm putting this on your tab, Cutlip."

Cutlip came up raging from the stone table, his big fists clenched at his sides. "I'm getting mighty sick of your big mouth, Long. You want me to break it up into strips?"

"No fightin' in here," Haswell said. "I don't have no fightin' in here.

The two bully boys stared at the big man on his knees, securing the length of chain to Longarm's ankle irons. They laughed, looked at each other, then shrugged. "You best learn to be a leetle more friendly, Haswell," Cutlip advised him.

Haswell didn't look up from his work. "I'm friendly enough, Brother Cutlip. It's just I don't want fightin' in my shop." He got up, slapping dust from the knees of his butternut pants. He nodded to Longarm. "Walk," he said.

Longarm took a step and pitched forward. He would have struck the ground on his face, but Haswell caught him and straightened him up. He said, "You can't take full steps no more."

Gowdy laughed. "He'll learn, Haswell. Let him learn."

Longarm learned fast. The length of chain between those ankle irons was short enough that he could not take a full-length stride. He could not walk properly at all; when he moved, he had to shuffle his feet.

"That's great," Cutlip said. "You learn fast, Long." Then Cutlip glanced briefly toward the blacksmith. "Elder Waymeyer said he'll pay you for this job later. Just put it on his tab."

Haswell nodded, but the young blacksmith's gentle face looked bleak. Longarm felt that it was almost as if Cutlip had told Haswell he was never going to be paid, and that Haswell had known that already. Whether Haswell learned fast or slow about Elder Waymeyer and his bully boys, he learned.

With Gowdy driving and Cutlip riding shotgun, the weapon's snout fixed on Longarm in the wagon bed, they transported him to the fields a few miles from the center of town.

Gowdy pulled the horse in off the narrow road, beside a beetfield that stretched across twenty acres at least to a stand of corn that extended green for another quarter of a mile. In all that sun-seared distance there was not a single tree or scrap of shade.

Far down the road, three men worked silently. Beyond them, Longarm saw a farmhouse with other people, men and women, around it. There were no other workers in the beet field.

Gowdy and Cutlip swung down from the flat-bed wagon. "Get down, Long," Cutlip said. "This is where you work."

Longarm swung his legs over the tailgate. He pushed himself up painfully and went sprawling out into the roadway. Cutlip and Gowdy laughed.

"You ain't real graceful, Long," Gowdy said.

Longarm pushed himself up to his hands and knees, and spoke curtly across his shoulder. "You take these ankle bracelets off me, Gowdy, and I'll show you graceful."

Gowdy aimed a kick at him, but Longarm anticipated it and lunged away. He pushed himself up and braced himself, legs as far apart as the chain would allow.

"Take off your coat, Long," Cutlip ordered. "You ain't going to need it no more."

When Longarm didn't move fast enough to suit him, Cutlip caught the collar of Longarm's frock coat and yanked downward. Longarm struck on his knees as Cutlip pulled the coat from him, arms inside out.

"Not a bad-looking coat," Gowdy said. "Looks like it ought to fit me."

Cutlip hesitated, studying the jacket; then, deciding it was not worth fighting over, he tossed it to his partner.

Longarm stood massaging his wrists. Cutlip had removed the handcuffs, but the marks of the irons were there, and it felt like he was still wearing them. He watched Gowdy don his coat and look down at himself admiringly. "Little long in the arms," Gowdy decided. "But a hell of a lot better than the homespuns these rubes wear."

"And you wouldn't want it too good," Longarm said, "or your great Elder Noah might take it away from you."

Cutlip turned slightly and, without telegraphing his move, drove the rifle butt deeply into Longarm's gut. Longarm gasped and went staggering halfway across the roadway before he fell.

76

Cutlip glanced toward him. "That was just in case you take a notion to run."

Gowdy crossed the narrow, dusty, hard-packed lane. He caught Longarm's bicep and yanked him to his feet. When Longarm was standing, Gowdy half-turned away and then swung back, sinking his thick fist deep under Longarm's belt.

Longarm sprawled backward. This time he fell in the gully between the first rows of beets. Gowdy stood laughing down at him. "And that there, Long," Gowdy said, "was just in case you think about *anything*—except working your ass off."

Longarm supported himself on his elbow, staring up at Elder Waymeyer's chosen pair. "I'd hate to be you two bastards," he said. "You know fifty days don't last forever. I'll tell you boys, when I get out of these chains, I'm coming looking for you."

Cutlip and Gowdy looked at each other and laughed.

Cutlip reached into the flatbed wagon and took out a hoe and a rake. He threw the utensils at Longarm, who managed to roll away before he was impaled.

Gowdy said, "Fifty days ain't forever, Bales."

They laughed again. Bales Cutlip stopped laughing suddenly. He said, "On your feet, Long. You get to work. And you keep working. You let us worry about how long fifty days is."

"Yeah," Gowdy said, "maybe you'll find fifty days is a hell of a lot longer than you think right now."

"However long," Longarm said, "my memory is longer."

Cutlip had turned toward the wagon. Now he stopped and looked across his shoulder, at Longarm. "All right, Long—I'll just give you something to think about for the next fifty days."

"The next fifty *long* days." Gowdy nodded, pleased, his eyes rolling.

"Fifty days," Longarm said, pulling himself to his feet. He used the hoe handle as a support. "That's the sentence, boys."

"Is it?" Cutlip stared at him, his face savage. "Maybe you didn't listen up, Long. Sure, your sentence is fifty days. And you're paid a dollar a day to square your fine, right? Only Elder Noah Waymeyer is a busy man. He must have disremembered to tell you about that dollar credit a day you're gonna git."

"Yeah. He must of forgot to tell you." Gowdy's ugly face

77

twisted with a look of mock concern.

Holding his breath, Longarm watched the bully boys, waiting. Cutlip said, "He forgot to tell you, you don't stay in our nice comfortable jail for nothing. You think you get nice clean accommodations like that for nothing? And you'll eat down here at the Hill family farmhouse mornings and nights. But somebody has got to pay for the food you eat. You don't expect us to do that, do you?"

"You can't expect Elder Waymeyer to pay it for you," Gowdy said.

Cutlip nodded. "But somebody has got to pay it, Long."

"That somebody is *you*, Long," Gowdy said.

"Out of your dollar-a-day credit, Long, you are charged one dollar and a quarter—for your keep."

Gowdy smiled cheerfully. "So you can see it may take you a mite longer than fifty days to pay your way out of them leg irons."

Cutlip swung up onto the boot of the wagon. He sat with the gun across his knees. Gowdy went around the vehicle, took the reins in his fist, and stepped up to the seat beside Bales.

Longarm stood staring up at them. "You just going to leave me out here?"

"Why not?"

"You're not going to stay to guard me?"

"In this sun?" Cutlip said. "Are you crazy?"

Gowdy laughed. "Where the hell you figure to go, Long? You gonna shuffle off across them ranges in leg irons?"

Cutlip nodded his head, motioning Gowdy to move the horse away back toward Alamut. Then he touched Gowdy's arm and faced Longarm again. "And by the way, Long. Every night when the Hills bring you back into the jail, we ask 'em how much work you done that day. We been in this business a long time, Long. We know about what a man your size ought to git done in ten hours a day out here. You don't measure up, you get a touch of the bullwhip every blessed night till you do."

Gowdy turned the horse on the narrow lane, and slapped the reins across the animal's sweated rump. He shouted back across his shoulder, "Makes you stop and think, don't it, Long?"

* * *

78

Longarm worked slowly, hoeing the weeds away from the young beet plants. The sun blazed down. In the unrelenting heat, he began to feel nauseated.

He kept working, moving slowly toward the brink of the rows. In the distance he saw the farmers, and the thin rise of smoke from the Hill farmhouse.

No one came near him. Infrequently, birds passed between him and the sun.

The blaze of heat struck him savagely. His legs felt weak, and he was afraid he would fall. His head and shoulders burned as if they were aflame.

Finally he could see nothing ahead of him except a blazing sunspot. Even when he closed his lids, the sunspot flared behind his eyes.

"Mister . . ."

Longarm heard the voice and jerked his head up. At first, all he saw was the vast sunspot, as if the earth itself were afire. Then the girl took vague shape in it, a dark blur wearing a blazing halo.

"Mister?"

Longarm supported himself on the hoe. Sweat ran down his dirt-streaked face and burned into his eyes. He felt the marble-sized droplets form along his hairline and rush, wet and hot and salty, across his fiery skin.

He blinked hard, and when he opened his eyes, the girl was extending him a wide, floppy-brimmed straw bonnet.

"Elder Regis Hill says you best wear this here hat before you end up with sunstroke."

Longarm nodded, thanking her. He placed the hat on his sunstruck head. Under the downturned straw brim, it seemed abruptly ten degrees cooler.

"Thank you," he said. "I mean if you're real—not just some mirage."

"You might have sunstroke, mister. None of us doubt that, out in this sun with no hat. But I ain't no mirage—whatever that is."

He smiled, leaning on the hoe. "That's funny. You look like a mirage."

"You talk real strange, don't you?"

Under the floppy hatbrim, his sun-fried eyes recovered their sight. They widened. They liked what they saw. Longarm didn't blame them.

This girl hadn't reached her twenties yet, but she was on her way in one hell of a hurry. She wasn't too tall, but every inch counted. She wore no makeup, and yet her lips were as red as if she'd been eating cherries, and her wide-set eyes were almond-shaped and deep brown, but they smoldered hotly, as if the sun burned in them too.

She was slender, but her hips were ample, straining against the drab fabric of her homespun dress. And that dress—it was as if it were already two sizes and two years too small for her, and she hadn't noticed and no one had wanted to tell her.

Her breasts were high and full, and they stood up brashly, even though she plainly wore nothing to support them under that somber dress. Her skin, throat, arms, and hands were burned a golden brown, with small, faint freckles that looked as if they'd be hot to the touch.

Under her straw bonnet, her hair was just slightly too dark to be called flaxen, and yet it was brightly blonde, sun-toasted. It reached almost to her shoulders in soft, careless ringlets.

In her shadowed face there seemed something smoldering, as if she were a faithful Mormon woman, but under her shyness burned an inexpressible and sullen defiance. Her world wasn't yet what she wanted it to be, something in that pouting face said, and everybody around her had better look out, because she was a girl who'd move hell to get what she wanted.

Longarm still couldn't believe she was real. His lips parted and he gazed at her, enchanted, gape-mouthed. His blood was boiling now in a way the sun had nothing to do with.

He shook his head. There was something faintly familiar about her, though he knew he'd never seen her before.

He realized at last that she was carrying a covered jug and a basket of food. She was not only heavenly and unearthly, she was an angel of mercy.

"God," he said, "I hope you're real."

"What do you mean?" She laughed up at him. "Of course I'm real."

"I think you're a vision."

"You can touch me if you want to."

He smiled. "I still wouldn't believe it. What's a beautiful girl like you doing in a godforsaken place like this?"

"Not very much," she conceded, with that go-to-hell look burning deeply in those hot, shadowy eyes.

"You mean you live here?"

She laughed again. "I'm Chastity's sister."

"Chastity?" Then he realized; she was plain Chastity McFee's sister, with enough loveliness for both of them.

"Purity?" he said, grinning. "Or maybe Charity. I hope Charity."

She laughed, shaking her head. "You talk so strange I don't know what you're saying."

"Words aren't important," he told her.

"I'm Consequence," she said. "Consequence Knight. Everybody calls me Connie. Elder Waymeyer wants to marry me. He said he had a celestial vision and God told him to marry me. I told them I'd kill myself first."

"I thought everybody here had to obey the word of the Elders."

She sighed, shaking her head. "Well, they might make me marry him, but I'm going to have myself some fun first."

"If your card ain't all filled up, put me down for a couple," Longarm said.

She frowned up at him; she obviously had no idea what he was talking about.

He laughed. "Oh, that's right. Dancing. That's a sin, ain't it?"

"An abomination before God," Connie said. "Right along with smoking and drinking and stealing." She did a little dance step.

He grinned. "Then you wouldn't know about filling in your dance card with the names of all the fellows who want to dance with you."

Connie sighed and shook her head. "I brought you some food," she said. "Mother Hill fixed it. And a jug of cold well water. But Elder Hill warns you that you better drink it slow. You drink it fast, it could make you sick. Really sick."

He gazed down at her. "And I don't want to get sick right now, do I?"

She smiled up at him. "Why, you're real nice. I was kind of scared to come out here alone. But you are nice." She looked around. "Why don't we go over to the edge of the corn rows? There's a little shade. Not much. You'll be cooler while you eat your lunch."

"I can only shuffle. I don't look so great trying to walk." He glanced toward the distant farmhouse. "And how about Elder Hill? What will he say if he doesn't see me working?"

"Oh, you don't have to worry about Elder Hill. Why, he's one of the nicest people you'll ever know. Next to Chastity's husband, Abel, I reckon Elder Hill is the nicest." As he shuffled along the row toward the thin line of shade at the corn rows, she said in a thoughtful tone, "Most of these people are nice. Oh, they are, when you get to know them. Good, simple people. Or they were, before Noah Waymeyer became head of the Council."

He flopped down in the slender shaft of shade, and took the earthenware jug from her. He removed his hat, poured the chilled well water into his cupped hand, and doused it on his forehead and face. Then he took a small sip, washed out his cottony mouth, and spat it out, aware that Connie watched him, unblinking.

"I was born here in Alamut," she said. "When they told me you were a Gentile from the outside, I was scared of you. All my life I've believed that you Gentiles had pointy tails and horns."

He smiled. "Well, I got to admit to a sort of horn."

But she was far too unworldly even to suspect what he was talking about. She just smiled at him. "I don't see it," she said. "You look like all the other men I know. Maybe taller. And prettier."

"Did anybody ever tell you how pretty you are, Connie?"

She caught her breath. "Oh, no. That would be a sin. Vanity. That's a sin."

"They should tell you," he said. He opened the napkin-covered hamper and found ripe peaches, cold meat, cheese, and fresh bread. His mouth watered, even though all his senses were concentrated at this moment in his loins. "A pretty young girl like you, somebody should tell you how lovely you are. All the time. They owe it to you."

"The Elders say beauty is a curse for women. Beauty hides the true worth underneath. Beauty passeth, they say, and if a woman believes too much in her beauty, she will have nothing left when it is gone."

"But she could have a hell of a time while she's got it."

She giggled and sat beside him in the shade. She took up one of the fresh peaches and munched on it, the juices dripping from the corners of her full mouth. Longarm felt himself growing harder even when he tried to think of something else. She said, "You know—that's what I think sometimes, lying alone in my bed. I tell myself I want a good time, and I could have it too. I think about the fun I could have—the men I could tease and touch and laugh with—before I'm old and ugly like these other women. Before I forget how to laugh." She trembled visibly. "Before I have to marry Elder Noah Waymeyer."

"God forbid," he said.

She shook the unpleasant prospect of forced marriage from her mind. "I think about the fun I could have—when I'm lying alone in bed—and sometimes I get so excited, so hot and burning, that I can't stand it."

He smiled at her, holding her gaze with his. "What do you do when you feel like that?"

Her face flushed red to her flaxen hair, and she stared at her clenched hands. "Oh, I couldn't tell you that," she said. "I couldn't tell anybody. Ever." She swallowed hard and looked around, eyes wide. "Nobody ever talked to me about such private things—ever. You better eat your lunch."

"I'm not very hungry right now. It can wait."

She tried to smile. She set aside more than half of the unfinished peach. "I'm not very hungry, either." She looked around. "Maybe you ought to rest."

"I'm resting. Looking at you rests me."

Her voice sounded odd. She tried to meet his gaze, but could not. "I mean . . . you could lie down . . . in the shade . . . in the corn rows."

His heart lunged, but he spoke doubtfully. "What about Elder Hill and those others—if they don't see me in the beet field?"

She sighed. "Elder Hill said I was to tell you, don't work so hard in this sun. He said to tell you the beet field will be here long after you're gone."

"God knows, I hope so."

"Go inside the corn rows," she whispered. "Lie down. Rest."

He watched her, but she would not look up at him. He moved back, wriggling between the corn rows. After a moment there was a rustling of corn stalks; she had followed him.

She stood up above him, staring down at him. She whispered. "Do you like to look at me?"

"My God."

"Do you think I'm pretty?"

"You're beautiful, Connie. A hell of a lot more beautiful

than any reflection has ever told you."

She hesitated a long time, then she reached down and caught the shapeless dress below her knees and slowly pulled it upward.

Longarm caught his breath. She wore no underthings. The faint flaxen triangle of her femininity gleamed wetly between her thighs. Her slim legs were shapely and long.

She stood there, holding the dress, letting him look at her, wanting him to enjoy her beauty.

He reached up and pressed the flat of his hand against her inner thigh. He moved upward and parted her hot, liquid lips with his finger.

He moved his two middle fingers in a slow, circular motion.

"Oh, my God," she whispered. "Oh, that feels so good."

She parted her legs, almost as if involuntarily, and sank down beside him. He kept his hand on her, but hesitated. "Are you—a virgin, Connie?"

She drew a deep breath, sighed, and shook her head. "One of the Elders," she whispered. "A long time ago. One Sunday afternoon. I was at home alone, and—"

"It's all right, then," he said. "Anyhow, if you are going to be Noah Waymeyer's wife, I owe it to you to take all I can from you."

"Yes." She slipped the old dress over her head, taking her straw hat along with the garment. The flaxen hair spilled back across her naked shoulders. He had never seen such fresh young loveliness.

He took her breast in his hand. With part of his mind he wondered how he was going to accomplish very much with his legs chained and shackled. But he was sure as hell going to find out.

It was as if she read his thoughts. Her head back, she gasped with delight as he nursed her nipple. Her slender hips began to whip back and forth, faster and faster.

"It doesn't matter if your legs are chained," she whispered in delight. "Mine aren't."

"Thank God," he whispered back.

Still working his fingers between her parted thighs, he shifted her so she knelt across him. "I don't think we ought to wait anymore."

"No. No. Please. Don't wait anymore."

With his left hand he jerked open the buttons on his fly.

When his staff hove into view, he heard her gasping cry of delight. "Oh, my God," she whispered. "It's beautiful. It's the most beautiful thing I ever saw." She laughed in a wild madness. "It looks good enough to eat."

"It is," he told her, "but not right now."

"Anything." She pressed her mouth over his, her tongue tasting his mouth. "Anything you want."

He took her hips in his hands and settled her down upon his throbbing colossus. She gasped for breath. Suddenly her hands gripped his shirt and she bucked insanely, crying out, whimpering, whispering.

Long before he reached the point of no return, it was already too late for her. She thrust herself upon him, wailing, flailing her hips, and then lying suddenly still, as if dead.

"I'll take care of you," she whispered, "in just a minute."

"Sure you will." Still thrust inside her, he began to nurse her breasts again, to enjoy the shapely contours of her body. She responded, going wild again. In less than three minutes she was whipping her hips frantically upon him, sobbing out her pleasure. This time she managed to wait for him, and they sagged together, spent, in the darkness of the shaded corn row.

It was hotter than the hole beyond hell in there, but Connie didn't notice, and he didn't care. He sprawled there and she lay upon him, her hand clutching him, her fingers moving as if she could not love him enough.

"Rest," Connie said. "You try to rest."

Rest was the last thought in his mind at this moment. He didn't know when he would see Connie again, and he believed he owed it to her and to her future husband, the Elder Waymeyer, to enjoy her as long as he could, as much as possible. Every time he gave it to Connie, he was really giving it to old Noah. Only it felt a hell of a lot better this way.

She held him with her delicate fingers, massaging with a gentleness that was calming and yet passionate and exciting. He could feel the desire that raged in her body, making her quiver, making the tips of her fingers like chips of ice on his hot flesh.

He laughed lightly. "We're in a hell of a fix—if they catch us like this."

She nodded, eyes glittering, and her moving hand gripped him tighter. "Yes. They might catch us." Her hand moved faster. "That only makes it all the more exciting, doesn't it?"

"I don't need any more excitement than your body," he said.

"Then do it," she said.

Driving himself to her, Longarm grinned tautly. She was more excited than he could have hoped she would be. No matter how furiously he wanted her, her own desire burned hotter. It might not always be true, but it was true at this moment, and he had only to enjoy it. Whatever he wanted from her, he would have and she would give willingly, anxiously, passionately.

She clung to him, trembling with anticipation and desire. A fine mist of perspiration accented her delicate features and held her ringlets plastered wetly against her forehead. Her eyes were half closed. Her nostrils flared and she panted through her open mouth.

He pulled her head down to his and kissed her parted lips, feeling the heat of her tongue, the sweet hotness of her mouth opening under his, wider and wider, as if she wanted to take all of him inside her.

They spun in the breathless heat of a blast furnace, and their bodies fused together. Her slender arms closed about him like metal bands that could not have been broken even if the whole valley rushed upon them. And, God knew, he expected them at any second, led by raging old Noah himself.

Yet he did not move away. He thrust harder. All he was thinking was, *What a hell of a way to die.*

She talked wildly, words spilling across her lips in hot madness, not making sense but increasing the fierce urgency in both of them.

He did not know how long he was with her this time. Everything lost meaning except their bodies fighting to become one. He felt Connie rise to a fevered pitch, her body wrenching fiercely; he heard her crying out, but she did not fall away. She only smashed herself more tightly against him, as if the appetites and compulsions he whetted in her willing body could never be sated.

She sank at last to exhaustion ahead of him, crying out wildly, and as he worked, she rose with him again, and then she sprawled helpless against him, and for a long time neither of them moved.

After a long time, she whispered against his face, "Oh,

wonderful, wonderful," she whispered. "Would you please tell me something?"

"Anything. What do you want me to tell you?"

"What's your name?"

Chapter 7

From the moment Longarm first sat down to supper at the table in the kitchen of the Hill family home, he found a stunning difference between the way the three formidable Hill men behaved outside this home and inside it. In the community and in his fields and barnyard, Elder Regis Hill was master of his world. His sons walked in his shadow. They spoke and others leaped to obey them. They were leaders in the valley, listened to, respected, and even feared.

Inside this house, it was different. Whether the Hill men admitted it to themselves or not, they lived by the rules of one woman. Clara Hill's tongue was sharp, her mind quick, and her laws rigid.

In a way it was amusing to see the way the father and two sons cringed under the lashing of Mother Hill's tongue, or retreated before the fire of her pale eyes.

Tension crackled in the big kitchen tonight. Longarm could feel it snapping almost like lightning before a storm. All three of the Hill men knew it too.

Mother Hill tried to look pleasant, but this was not easy. Like most Mormon wives and mothers, she was no beauty in the first place, and anger had stiffened the heavy features of her face, made her thin lips hard, straight lines, and turned her eyes to small chips of blue ice.

Connie Knight moved wraithlike, helping Ma Hill serve the heavy, steaming evening meal, or sat silently in her chair, hands folded in her lap.

Damn, she was a lovely little package. But he warned himself he had to be careful. Connie worked here; she had come to the Hill place after her older sister married Elder Abel McFee. At first the Hills had thought maybe Consequence would marry one of the Hill sons, until God had chosen her for Elder Noah Waymeyer himself in a celestial revelation.

Most Mormon women looked like Clara Hill or Chastity McFee, and not at all like the delicate and lovely Connie. The Mormons would tell you that beauty wasn't the first consideration with *their* women. "With us," a Mormon had told Longarm, "it ain't how pretty a woman is. It's how good she is in the house and how she fits in with the other wives and how well she pleases her husband after a long day that matters. And if she pleasures her man as she should, he won't ever go sniffing off after some pretty face. If she does her wifely chores right, he won't stray. He won't have the time, and he won't have the inclination."

Clara Hill looked like the women Mark Twain had discovered on a visit to Salt Lake City. Twain said Mormon women were so homely that anyone marrying one of them performed an act of Christian charity, and the world should bow in dumb admiration of the poor son of a bitch who married sixty of them. Longarm admitted that old Sam Clemens hadn't been too far from the sad truth. The cold severity in most of the women matched their attire and their glum outlook on the world around them. Clara Hill appeared to have been made in the Mormon female mold. But sitting in sedate modesty at the table was her exact opposite, the rebellious and defiant Consequence.

As the Hill men bent over their plates to eat, Mother Hill stood back from the table, hands on her hips.

Her voice was a model of calm rectitude. "So we had company today, Elder Hill?"

Elder Regis Hill winced and glanced up. He swallowed twice at his boiled potato and managed to nod. "Yes, Mother. Elder Noah Waymeyer did come on out here in the middle of the afternoon. I thought maybe he had come to visit

Consequence. After all, he is trying to persuade her to be his wife—"

"His *seventh* wife," Connie chimed in. "I'll never marry that evil old man. I swear. I'll die first."

"Now, Consequence," Elder Hill said, glad to escape for a moment from his wife's righteous wrath. "We must not oppose the will of our God, who has given us so much."

"I'm not against God," Connie said.

"Elder Waymeyer is God's leading apostle among us, Consequence. His word is God's word," Regis Hill said.

Longarm felt the defiant little Connie was about to blurt out that she would believe this when she heard it from God Himself, but whatever she might have said was lost in the sharp crackle of Ma Hill's voice in the silent room.

"Never mind Consequence, Elder Hill. God will provide the right answer for Consequence when the time comes. You know very well why Elder Waymeyer came out here this afternoon. Just as you know it had nothing to do with Consequence, though he did stare at her with cow eyes."

Elder Hill cleared his throat. "Well, yes, the Elder and his helpers did come out. To collect our tithe."

"How many times a year does he collect from us?"

"Mother, we all must tithe."

"We tithe more than our share. It is more like stealing."

"Mother! That is sacrilegious. Don't say such things."

"I speak the truth, Elder Hill," Mrs. Hill said. "I have no fear of God. God is a just God. And God knows I speak the truth."

"Mother. Elder Waymeyer explained to the boys and me. Didn't he, Ned? Ezekiel? What was it Elder Waymeyer said? It is the need of the community, Mother. Those of us who have more—"

"Have more because we work harder. We produce more. To tithe is one thing. To support Elder Waymeyer and his cronies in sinful luxury is something else. It is an abomination before God."

"Mother. You must not say such things. The community needs—"

Her voice lashed out at her husband and he cringed under it. "The community had plenty before Elder Waymeyer was named spiritual leader of our Council—"

"You must not talk like this, Mother. You must not. We must obey the rules of our Council."

Longarm said, "I know I'm new here. But in other Mormon settlements, tithing is ten percent, isn't it?"

"That's right." Clara Hill's voice crackled.

"And yet Elder Waymeyer takes more?" Longarm inquired.

"More and more." Mrs. Hill prowled the room. "He does not take a tithe, he takes substance itself, food from our mouths."

"Why do you tolerate it?" Longarm asked, keeping his voice low and devoid of passion.

"Elder Waymeyer is our leader," Elder Hill said.

"But why do you let him take more than God's fair share?" Longarm asked, puzzled.

"That is the very question I want answered," Clara Hill said.

Elder Regis Hill pushed himself back in his chair, a broad-shouldered man with a kindly face, deeply troubled, but fighting to remain true to Mormon covenants.

"I am shocked that Mother Clara would speak this way," he said. "She has given her life to our Church, our way, and our God—"

"And now must I give the food off my table, the clothes off my back?" she demanded.

Elder Hill continued to address Longarm, obviously trying to avoid further confrontation with his angry wife.

"You can be forgiven for questioning our ways, Mr. Long," Hill said, "because you are a stranger, an outsider, and your education has been left incomplete. One might almost believe that the Angel Moroni sent you to us to be instructed. You will be forced to work hard here in Alamut, but you will learn that it is from hard work and devotion—from discipline—that even arid earth can be brought to fruitfulness. And only thus.

"You see, Mr. Long, we of the Boulder Canyon country are adherents to the fundamental religious beliefs of the original Church of Jesus Christ of Latter-Day Saints. We trust the teachings as revealed by God Himself through revelations to Joseph Smith at Fayette, New York, in 1830. That means we of Alamut Valley remain faithful to the words of Joseph Smith in every sense of that law."

"I have no argument with that," Clara Hill said. "I question these new leaders, not the teachings of the old."

"Our new leaders must be as sacred to us as Joseph Smith

and his first Church Council. It was not easy for them, any more than for those who followed Brigham Young and the Council of the Twelve Apostles in that terrible trek overland to Salt Lake Valley. We here follow the teachings of those original Apostles. We are faithful to the words of Brigham Young. We live according to *The Book of Mormon, Doctrines and Covenants,* and *The Pearl of Great Price.* This means, Mr. Long, we do not select what we believe—we adhere to *all* the rules of the Church and of its leaders."

Though Longarm felt an inner excitement, a new hope, as if he glimpsed a faint light at the end of a long tunnel, he kept his voice mild and inquiring. "Still, like Mother Hill asks, if the leaders take advantage of you, ain't there anything you can do about it?"

Elder Hill nodded. "Of course there is. The Council of Elders will hear complaints, and will act upon them."

Longarm frowned. "But they allowed Elder Waymeyer to put out Elder Abel McFee and his wives when the Elder went against them in my so-called trial."

"Elder McFee will be all right," Elder Hill said.

"I pray to God that he will be safe," Mrs. Hill said.

"Abel McFee will be all right." Connie spoke suddenly, her voice assured. "He is a gentle man, but nobody will push him too far."

"Still, there is the old resentment between Elder McFee and Elder Waymeyer," Clara Hill reminded them.

"There is none. Not on the side of Abel McFee," Regis Hill protested. "He would have been leader of our Council, that's true. But when the Council selected Elder Waymeyer, Abel accepted the choice calmly. And Abel knows, as you seem not to know, that we of the community keep a rein on our leaders. They know it."

"What kind of rein do you have on Elder Waymeyer?" Clara Hill demanded.

"That's a fair question, Elder Hill," Longarm said in his most disarming voice. "From what I hear, Elder Waymeyer does what he wants. He takes from you people according to his own rules. In return, what does he give you?"

Clara nodded emphatically. "That is the very question I would like to hear answered."

"Elder Waymeyer carries out what he sees as best for our people, our Church, our valley. As long as he does these things,

93

we must respect and obey him. This is as true as the fact that we live totally according to the rules of our Holy Church. We believe the priestly power comes to our spiritual leaders directly from the original three of Christ's own Disciples.

"This has brought us the Thirteen Articles of Faith by which we are guided. Trust and respect for our Church and its Apostles are part of our religion. We must not rebel against the leaders of our community. This valley—as we have built it from barren wastes—can persist and thrive and grow only as long as we have strong leaders and as long as we follow their instructions. I say that Elder Waymeyer is that strong leader and that we owe him our allegiance, and that we say no more on the subject."

The supper ended in tension and silence. Afterwards, Elder Hill and his older son drove Longarm in to the town jail. As they drove, Elder Hill said, "One must understand the strange circumstances of this valley, and how our people splintered away from the Church in Salt Lake City—and came here to follow the dictates of our conscience and the teachings of Brigham Young.

"My parents, and those like them, refused to obey the laws of the Gentile United States against plural marriage. They could no longer stay with the main body of the Church, which agreed to live according to laws imposed from outside our Church. They removed themselves to this valley. It was desert wasteland then. They brought water and flowers and food. We have prospered. We have worshipped our God Almighty according to the dictates of our own conscience—without interference by outside laws, local, state, or national."

"And Elder Waymeyer doesn't put new restrictions on you?" Longarm asked.

"None." Elder Hill spoke much more forcefully away from the kitchen where his wife ruled. "We are a splinter group from the old Mormon Church. We hold to its fundamental teachings. But we left Salt Lake Valley—or my parents did—in bitterness. The Mormons of Salt Lake called our parents devils and shunned them. They spitefully called our community Alamut—"

"Ain't Alamut a name like Zion—from the Good Book?" Longarm asked, though he was certain it was not. That name had troubled him from the first.

"No. The name Alamut was given us in contempt. We have worn it defiantly—and proudly."

"Where did the name come from?" Longarm asked.

"From the mountain stronghold of the Assassins. That's what conservative Mormons called our people when they broke away. Alamut was originally the mountain stronghold of a secret order of religious fanatics in Persia. It was from there that the 'Old Man of the Mountains,' as he was called by the Crusaders, led forces to terrorize the invading Christians. These people of Alamut were ready to die in blind obedience to their leader. For that reason we have been proud to call this village and valley Alamut. We are faithful."

They approached the town jail in the gathering darkness. Longarm asked, "And so Elder Waymeyer and Elder McFee were once candidates for head of your Council?"

"That's right," Ezekiel said.

"They were both from the oldest families, I reckon?" Longarm prompted. "And so the choice was easy?"

Elder Hill drew a deep breath and spoke in a low tone. "It was not an easy choice. The McFees have been valley leaders for two generations. But many thought Abel too gentle, too easily swayed. Noah was strong. We chose the stronger man."

"And Noah has lived here all his life?"

"Oh, no," Ezekiel Hill said. "Elder Waymeyer came here ten years ago. He was made our Council leader that same year."

"He had every qualification," Elder Hill said in a sharp tone. "He came directly to us from Salt Lake City. He came from the Tabernacle itself to lead us."

"How lucky for you," Longarm said with an irony that he knew was lost on the rancher and his son.

"Yes," Elder Hill said. "We have been most fortunate. God watches over us closely."

"I hope so," Longarm said.

Longarm didn't sleep well that night. Someone had placed a flat straw mattress on the springs of the iron cot in the jail cell, and he undressed, lay down, and covered himself with the blanket. The desert night was cold, the sky through the barred door bright with stars.

Sleep eluded him. He had too much on his mind.

Noah Waymeyer. Thinking about the leading Elder of the

community, Longarm felt his stomach twist into knots, and his hands clench to hard fists.

So Noah was not a native of this valley. Why had he thought that the first moment he saw the Elder, without any evidence at all? Noah had shown up ten years ago—very likely along with Bales Cutlip and Gowdy—and had taken over the community of Alamut, displacing Abel McFee, who should have been named its spiritual leader.

And now, according to Clara Hill, who spoke the angry truth, Noah was bleeding them all dry.

Longarm twisted on the mattress in the darkness. The threat that troubled him most of all was the certain knowledge that despite the apparent lightness of the sentence for vagrancy imposed upon him by Elder Waymeyer, the man had no intention of allowing him to leave Alamut Valley alive.

He remembered the way Cutlip and Gowdy had laughed about the dollar a day that was supposed to pay his fine, but which really did not cover the cost of his keep. There was no way that he could work out his fine; his debt would pile higher against him every day he stayed here—or every day Noah Waymeyer let him stay.

He slept fitfully and awoke at the first grayness of dawn. The very walls of the small cell seemed to press in upon him. He felt as if he could not draw a full breath.

He swung his legs over the side of the cot and stood up carefully, remembering not to take more than half a step.

He shuffled across the rough flooring toward the wide, barred doorway. In the dim light he could see the rich Mormon valley, the carefully laid out farm plots, the slate ridges ringing them, and the distant, unnamed ranges far beyond—out there where freedom lay.

He stepped into the doorway and clutched the bars in his fists, pressing against the chill, damp metal.

He stared out at the open world, sucking in long, deep draughts of fresh air, his lungs aching.

A rifle cracked from the shadows of a building across the main street. The slug slammed into the adobe wall next to the door, peppering him with fragments of hard clay.

Longarm lunged backward in reflex. Forgetting the chain, he tried to take a full step. He was sent sprawling across the floor. He bumped his head hard and lay unmoving, swearing, his fists clenched on each side of him.

He heard the crowd gathering, men running across the yard in the early light. He did not move.

"It's the Gentile."

"Somebody shot at the prisoner."

"Is he dead?"

Somebody thrust the onlookers aside and unlocked the barred door. Longarm recognized Bales Cutlip's voice. "Is he dead?"

Cutlip and Gowdy entered the cell and knelt beside Longarm.

Longarm turned, gazing up at them blandly. "Funny, I figured you two might be nearby."

Cutlip said only, "We were on our way to take you to the farm to work. We heard the shot."

Longarm sat up. "I'll bet you did."

"You trying to say we had something to do with that bushwhacking?"

Longarm shrugged. When Cutlip would have helped him to his feet, Longarm shoved him aside and pulled himself up alone. He stared at Gowdy's shaggy, ugly face. *Somebody shot at me.*

"One thing you best make up your mind to, partner," Cutlip said. "Plenty of these people here hate you."

"Enough to kill me?"

Cutlip shrugged. "You're a stranger to them, hombre. A Gentile."

Longarm stared into Cutlip's deadly eyes. "And they want to kill me for that?"

Cutlip shrugged again. "For plenty of these good people — persecuted and cheated the way they been — you bein' a stranger and a Gentile is all the reason they need for blasting your head off."

When Connie came out into the blazing fields with water and lunch for him at noon, Longarm was still shaken inside, still jumping at shadows.

She tried to take his hand and lead him into the corn rows, her breath quickening. "Somebody tried to kill me this morning," he said.

She sighed and said, "There's nobody around now. Only us. I've thought of nothing but you."

"Listen to me, Connie. You can help me."

"I want to help you." She urged him again toward the corn rows.

"They mean to kill me. Either they don't want me to live because I'm some kind of threat to them, or somebody is jealous of what you and I did to the corn yesterday. Maybe they're afraid we'll wither the stalks."

She shook her head. "Nobody could know. Besides, nobody cares but Elder Waymeyer. And he's too busy piling up money to watch us. He knows that sooner of later I'll have to marry him. That's all he cares."

"We could run away."

"You know we couldn't do that. With those chains, you can barely make it to the corn rows."

"Damn it, Connie, will you listen to me? If Noah Waymeyer don't want me dead, tell me who else might. Is one of the Hill boys in love with you?"

"No. They're too scared of Elder Waymeyer to look my way."

"Who, then? Who, Connie?"

"There's nobody, I tell you."

"How about that blacksmith?"

"Martin?" Her lovely mouth twisted in disdain.

"Yeah. Haswell. He was out here before Elder Hill and Zeke took me in to the jail. He didn't come to see the Elder. Who'd he come to see? You?"

"Maybe." She shrugged. "You don't have to worry about Martin Haswell. He's been in love with me since I was about thirteen."

"We shouldn't have done that yesterday," Longarm said. "We had no right. I didn't know about Martin."

"What is there to know about Martin? Martin will never have me. He knows that. He's like some lovesick animal; he can't stay away from me. But he hasn't the courage to stand up against Elder Waymeyer."

As she spoke, she had been leading Longarm toward the corn rows. Now they were in among them, and he was still protesting, but he knew he wasn't going to resist her. She drove him out of his mind. No wonder poor old Martin Haswell hung around helplessly.

Inside the first row of corn, Connie reached down and jerked the buttons loose at his fly. She took his hardening staff in her hand, breathless. "Oh, I want it so bad," she whispered.

"Damn it. Listen to me."

But she slipped to her knees, her arms about his thighs, nuzzling and kissing him. She looked up, her eyes full of fire. She drew her tongue across him. "You like that. You know you like that, don't you?"

"Damn it. I like to live too. I'd like to get the hell out of here."

She stared up at him, her face bleak. "You know I can't help you."

"Why can't you? Get me a hammer and chisel. That's all I ask."

"You know I can't do that."

"For God's sake, why not? Hasn't anybody in this valley got enough sand to oppose Noah Waymeyer?"

"I'm not afraid of Elder Waymeyer." She lay back and drew him down to her.

"Then why won't you help me?"

"Because I don't want you to get away. I never met anybody like you before. I never will again. Nobody can do it like you. Nobody. Nobody else drives me right out of my mind so I can't stand it. If you got away, Custis, who'd be here to comfort me?"

Chapter 8

Suddenly, time itself whipped out of control.

In the remote, lost valley where time seemed only to plod forward, lose its way, and double back on itself, it was if the days raced past.

Each morning at daybreak, Bales Cutlip and fat-faced Gowdy arrived at the doors of the jail.

Cutlip unlocked the door and stepped cautiously and watchfully inside. Gowdy stood outside, on guard.

Each day, Longarm expected Cutlip to attack him, if for no better reason than that his shackled legs made him an almost helpless target.

Instead, Cutlip only jerked his head, ordering Longarm out to the waiting wagon.

It was the way they watched him that troubled Longarm. They studied him strangely, narrowly, almost as if amused.

One morning they reached the farm before Elder Hill and his sons had come out of the kitchen.

When Longarm stood to vault over the side of the wagon bed, Gowdy reached out with the butt of his rifle and shoved him suddenly.

Losing his balance, Longarm sprawled on the stone-hard ground.

The rear door of the house was thrown open, squealing on

its dry hinges. The entire Hill family, followed by Connie, came through the door. Mrs. Hill and Connie remained at the edge of the porch in the early-morning sunlight. But Regis Hill and his sons charged down the steps.

Old Hill looked like an avenging angel of God in his rage. "Here!" he shouted, shattering the stillness. "What is this?"

Longarm pushed himself to his knees and then stood, trying to dust himself off.

"What kind of cruelty is this?" Elder Hill demanded. His fiery gaze fixed first on Cutlip and then on Gowdy.

Gowdy shrugged. "It was an accident, Elder. That's all. I thought he was going to fall, so I tried to catch him."

"With the butt end of your rifle?" Zeke Hill said.

Cutlip stared murderously at the younger Hill, in a way he would not have dared confront the Elder.

"That's right. We thought he was falling. I told Gowdy to let him grab the rifle butt. He was too late, that was all."

Elder Hill stared coldly at the two plug-uglies. His gaze called them liars, but when he spoke, his voice was under control. "I hope you are telling the truth," he said. "If I see anything like this happen again, I shall report you both to the Council of Twelve."

Cutlip drew a deep breath, then answered defiantly, sure of himself, his position, and his orders from the leader himself. "You got good prison labor, Hill. For free. You want to lose your help, you just make trouble."

"Yeah." Gowdy nodded his shaggy head. "You don't want the Gentile, there's plenty other farms'll take him."

"You just think on that," Cutlip said. He slapped the reins, turning the horse. They sped away along the hard-packed lane toward the town of Alamut without looking back. Dust rose in beige clouds, glinting with shafts of sunlight, in their wake.

Longarm stared at the Hill men. "I'd better get to work."

"Are you sure you're all right?" Elder Hill insisted.

Longarm met the Elder's gaze levelly. "I don't want to make any trouble for you with your leader. A Gentile. An outsider. A prisoner. I ain't worth it."

Clara Hill came down the steps. With Connie on the other side of him, the motherly woman insisted upon helping him up the steps to the porch. "You come in and have coffee and eggs. There's plenty of time for work."

The Hill men followed silently. In the kitchen, Mrs. Hill

prepared a breakfast for Longarm. Connie got him a mug of steaming coffee. As he drank it, Connie got a warm damp cloth and wiped the dirt from Longarm's bruised face.

He grinned at her. "Almost worth getting beaten up for."

"They said it was an accident," Elder Hill said, his voice oddly empty.

Longarm's head jerked up. "And when some 'accident' kills me? Will you believe them then?"

"It could have been an accident," Elder Hill said stubbornly.

Longarm shrugged. "You believe what you want."

"Why would they want to kill you?" Ned Hill said. "That doesn't make sense. You are worth something to us alive. You can work. Dead, you are not worth anything to them."

"Maybe they'd feel safer with me dead," Longarm suggested.

"What kind of talk is that?" Regis Hill demanded.

"I don't know," Longarm said. "I know that shot somebody took at me was no accident. Trying to make me break my neck falling from that wagon was no accident, either."

"You still haven't said why they would want you dead," Ned Hill persisted.

"Because I don't *know* why. I can tell you this—if I could send three descriptions to the U.S. marshal's office in Denver, I'd stake my life I could come up with some interesting information on—"

"That's enough, sir!" Regis Hill's voice shook the dishes in the kitchen cabinet. "I am sorry. But I cannot tolerate your charges against our leader and his trusted workers. You have no proof, only suspicions. We are true Disciples in this house. We do not bear false testimony against our Elders." He drew his gaze across the faces of the people in the room. Even the willful Clara Hill lowered her eyes under the savage reproof in Elder Hill's flushed countenance.

A silence hung in the room. At last Regis Hill said, "You work well, Long. I have no complaint. But if you continue to make false charges against our leader, I myself shall condemn you before the Council of Twelve."

Longarm got up from the chair. For a moment he met and held the Elder's gaze. Then he shrugged and turned away. He shuffled across the room and pushed open the back door.

"Where are you going?" Clara Hill called. "Your breakfast is ready."

Longarm did not look back. "I'm not hungry," he said.

At noon, Connie came to the beet fields with well water and lunch. She smiled uncertainly at Longarm. "I know it's not worth anything. But I believe you."

"You've just got ants in your underdrawers." His voice was sour.

She laughed. "I don't wear underdrawers. You should know that by now."

"No." He stared down at her. "I shouldn't know anything about you."

"Why not?" she cried out. "I want you. I want no one else."

"That's because I'm easy to get. I'm here when you want me."

"Why are you so mad at me?"

He grinned faintly. "I'm sorry, Consequence. I'm not mad at *you*. But I'm too mad to be nice to anybody."

"I could soothe you."

"No. Not now. Not today. Not ever again."

She gasped in protest and clutched his arm, gripping it fiercely. "Why? Why do you have to treat me like this? Because you hate them?"

"I don't. It has nothing to do with them. Well, not directly. It's you I'm thinking about, Connie."

"You're thinking about me, but you don't want me?" She clung to his arm, staring up at him, hurt and puzzled. "I don't understand."

"I'm just not going to touch you again, Connie."

She shook her head, stunned. "Don't you—like it?"

Again he smiled, despite the rage churning in his belly. He sighed. "Next to breathing, Connie, I can't think of anything I'd rather do than make love to you."

"Then do it. Now. Anytime. Whenever you want. I'm willing. Why not?"

"Because it's too dangerous."

"I knew it was dangerous the first time; I don't care about that."

"*I* care."

"Are you afraid of them?"

"I'd be a fool not to be, given the circumstances. I'm almost helpless. I can't get away. They're just looking for some way to kill me so it looks accidental. Yeah, I'm scared. But I'm not talking about me. I'm talking about you. It's too dangerous for you."

"I don't care!"

"Well, I care. You won't help me get away—"

"I can't. You know I can't."

"And I can't stay here and maybe get you in trouble that you can't wriggle out of. They warned the Hills today about trying to defend me. Next they'll be condemning people seen even talking to me. That means you."

She sobbed suddenly, then straightened. "What will I do without you?"

"I don't know. You've made this hell bearable for me. I don't know what *I'll* do without *you*. But I know I am going to do without you, because I've got to be smart enough for both of us."

"What's smart about throwing me away? You can have me—anytime you want."

"That's because you're not smart."

"You do hate me."

"I don't hate you. I never will hate you, Connie. But you've got to be smart. If you're going on living among these religious fanatics, you've got to be smart, a hell of a lot smarter than you are."

"Oh? If I were smart, what would I do? Run and marry Noah Waymeyer?"

"Hell, no. If you were smart, you'd use all those wiles you use on me—on Martin Haswell. Do to him everything you've learned from me. And all those things you were born knowing. It looks to me like Haswell's your only chance to get out of marrying Noah Waymeyer."

"Even if I would—even if I could—Martin wouldn't dare touch me."

"Oh, come on, Consequence. I ain't one of these backwoods rubes. I know what you are, I know what you can do. And I also know there's no man in this valley—or maybe any other valley—who could resist if you offered it all to him."

"What would that get me?"

"I don't know. Maybe it would get you out of here. Maybe it would make Martin Haswell willing to fight for you."

"I could never do that. You're just trying to stir up trouble."

"All right. Don't do it. Go on like you are, and end up in old Noah's bed—along with his six smelly wives."

The next few days were quiet. Cutlip and Gowdy continued bringing Longarm to the farm to work, but they no longer stopped at the farmhouse. They drove him directly into the fields. They said little, watching him narrowly, and he stayed alert, watching them.

Each afternoon, Martin Haswell arrived at the Hill house, bathed, his beard trimmed and his hair combed.

Longarm watched Haswell and Connie. She did nothing, but Longarm grinned coldly. He could tell that inwardly she was thinking about what he had said to her. She was not going to do without loving any longer than she was forced to. And since he had, rightly or wrongly, truly opened her up to passion, it was harder than ever now for Consequence Knight to live without a man.

Climbing up into the Hills' open wagon to be driven in to the jail for the night, Longarm took one last look at Connie and Martin. He didn't give a damn about Martin Haswell, but he was condemned to spend the rest of his days in this Mormon valley unless he could stir up trouble between Noah Waymeyer and his flock. His best bet at this moment seemed to be Martin Haswell and Consequence Knight.

But the hell of it was, you didn't make a stud horse out of a docile jackass. At least not overnight.

And Longarm had the feeling that time was running out—for Connie, for Martin, and for himself.

The days passed, one after another. The Hill family was concerned, friendly, yet withdrawn, as if afraid to trust any feeling of friendliness toward the Gentile. And Connie watched Longarm sullenly, angrily, and yet waiting for him to nod toward her.

Each morning at daybreak, Longarm was transported by Cutlip and Gowdy out into the remote regions of the vast Hill farm. They rode silently in the sweet, cool dawn.

Longarm watched the sun glow opal and jade above the bronze sandstone slopes. Put out of the wagon far from the house each morning, he worked slowly, gazing up at those ridges where lichens grew and pale, nameless flowers bloomed like a distant promise of freedom. The fresh daylight touched at the heavy shoulders of weathered rocks on those ragged heights. He stared up at those plateaus, wanting to climb them, to lose himself up there, to run, even chained, toward the freedom the heights and lonely places promised.

Cutlip had put him out at the last corn row, almost in the shadow of a sandstone cliff.

"Work your way back to the house," Cutlip told him. "That way we can check on what you're doing."

"You mean you don't take Elder Hill's word for my work?" Longarm inquired.

"You just do your work, Gentile," Cutlip replied, "and let us worry about who we can trust."

Longarm chopped slowly at the earth, thinking the same thoughts over and over, as if his mind were on a treadmill. Had Billy Vail sent anyone to look for him? The job he'd been sent on was only supposed to take him a couple of days; by this time, an entire platoon of federal marshals should be looking for him. For all the good that would do, he mused bitterly; they wouldn't easily find him in this place.

The silence of the valley pressed down upon him. At least he was shielded from the sun by the looming cliffs, but the silence, the windless silence, reinforced his loneliness. No breeze moved through the endless rows of corn to rustle the leaves and tassels; no bird sang.

Then, above him, high among the sandstone cliffs, there was a faint *click,* the ticking of stone on stone. He straightened, frowning. Had he imagined it? No; there it was again, louder, and yet again, and suddenly it was a sustained rattling, and then a roar. All around him he began to hear the thudding of heavy stones on soft earth, and the fibrous crashing and tearing of cornstalks under an increasing barrage of falling rocks.

As rapidly as he could, hobbled by the chain between his ankle irons, using his hoe to support himself, Longarm shuffled away from the base of the cliff, protecting his head as well as he could with his free arm, tripping and falling, and finally crawling through the rows, heading toward the narrow lane. Even in his panic, he knew that cliff couldn't suddenly hurl stones of its own volition. But someone on those heights could send rocks and stones bounding down the precipice and into the high rows of corn.

He lunged to his feet and stared upward toward the heights. More rocks struck the field, thumping and rolling through the thick growth of corn.

He caught the shadow of movement. Someone was up there.

Longarm didn't wait to see who that man on the heights might be. He broke once again into a hobbling run, moving as swiftly as the short chain would permit. Behind him the avalanche had slowed, but it had not stopped. Bounding rocks spun downward along the sheer cliff, struck projecting stone, and bounced outward like some guided projectiles.

The stalks of corn shook and bent and broke under the assault. Other rocks bounded down. A boulder as large as a cask flashed in the sunlight as it swerved out from the shadows into the clear air over the field. Dust, in a writhing mass, followed the avalanche downward, enveloping the lethal boulders until they leaped free, spinning outward into the corn rows.

Coming out of the end of the row to the ditch at the side of the hard-packed lane, Longarm was thrown prostrate. The thundering, clattering rockfall slowed, but the rumbling echoed in the still, terrible morning.

Using the hoe handle to propel himself, Longarm swung up to his feet. He glanced back toward the rim of the cliff. As the panic subsided inside him, Longarm realized that only a miracle had saved his life in that field. In the hot, bare road, he gasped for breath, as if he had not breathed for long, painful minutes.

Dazed, he shuffled along the road toward the Hill home. He didn't look back again. All he could think was that he had to get out of there.

Suddenly Longarm was aware of a stinging sensitivity in the middle of his back. He felt as if he wore a bullseye between his shoulder blades. Anyone who wanted to kill him from the rim of that cliff would find him a tempting target in the middle of the open road, in easy range for any rifle.

He winced, waiting, still shuffling as swiftly as he could in the glinting dust, but no more sounds came from the top of the steep bluff.

His heart quieted, and his reason returned. They weren't going to shoot him unless it could be made to look accidental, or like the work of some sorehead Mormon with a deep, abiding, and unyielding hatred for Gentiles.

They had tried to kill him with that manmade avalanche; he had not the least doubt of that. He felt weakness in the backs of his legs, and his mind spun at the thought of the near misses he'd somehow managed to live through in that field.

Cutlip and Gowdy. There was no question in his mind but

that they were working on direct orders from Noah Waymeyer himself. It was the work of the bully boys, that avalanche, he was certain. They had deposited him right where they wanted him, in the first row of corn under the sandstone rim. They had gone away and left him there, and then the rocks had started raining down on him.

If they had killed him, it would have been regrettable, but it would have looked like an act of God.

Longarm swore. Old Regis Hill had to listen to him now.

Shambling along the road, he tried to put some sense into these attacks, these attempts to cause his "accidental" death.

If Noah Waymeyer and his bully boys wanted him dead so fiercely, why didn't they just execute him and get it over with?

Well, there was no doubt they wanted him dead. But for some reason desperately important to them, they wanted his death to look like an accident. They wanted to be able to call it an accident before the Council of Twelve, and they wanted to be believed.

Why did they care? Something important to them hinged on his death, on his never being permitted to leave this valley alive. But of equal importance to them was that his death look like a genuine accident to the disciples.

It occurred to him that in the past ten years there must have been others who wandered into the valley, saw too much, remembered too much, and posed some threat to Waymeyer's rule. Maybe those other executions had been sloppily carried out. Maybe the Council of Twelve had warned their leader that such brutality was not to be tolerated, even in the reigning Elder!

Now that made sense. And that was a little good news in with the bad. It meant that Noah and his plug-uglies, while they ruled and misruled the valley, didn't yet have total command, after all.

They had to answer to somebody—likely the other Elders. And they couldn't get away with another murder.

He tried to walk faster in the blaze of morning sunlight. His thoughts raced ahead of him, and again he began to hope. That light at the end of the tunnel looked as big as a gold double eagle at the moment.

Among these ignorant, backcountry farmers, there must be some with common sense and an understanding of fair play, fair-minded men who had been pushed, and who were on guard.

If such men existed, who were they? How could he find them before Noah and his boys worked out a foolproof accidental death for him?

Who would listen to him?

Stumbling along the road, Longarm saw that Elder Hill and his sons had leaped into a wagon and were racing toward him. His pulse quickened. Elder Hill had wanted hard evidence. Well, he had it for them today.

Elder Hill was handling the reins. He pulled the wagon up beside Longarm. Ned and Zeke leaped to the ground and helped Longarm onto the wagon bed.

"What happened?" Zeke asked. "You look as white as milk! What's wrong?"

Longarm stared at them. "They tried to kill me again," he said.

He saw the way old Regis Hill withdrew. The farmer's beard seemed to stiffen, and his mouth pulled into a taut line.

Longarm's voice hardened. "I've got proof for you this time, Elder Hill. The hard evidence you said you had to see."

"It sounded like thunder down here," Ned said as the wagon moved more slowly now toward the sandstone cliff. "Like a storm with the sun shining bright."

"It was no storm," Longarm said. "It was an avalanche— from that ridge up there." He spoke stubbornly, knowing that Hill was opposing him silently. "A manmade avalanche."

Though his legs were shackled, Longarm was the first off the wagon when Regis Hill pulled to a stop in the shadow at the base of the cliff.

Longarm led them into the shattered rows of corn.

He stared at Regis, his eyes cold and a muscle working in the hard line of his jaw. "Crows didn't do that," he said.

Expressionlessly, Regis strode along, assessing the damage done by the rocks and boulders.

"They did it," Longarm said, staring straight at Regis.

The Elder heeled around, locking his gaze hard against Longarm's. "They?" he said. "Who do you mean, Long?"

"I don't mean the crows, Elder," Longarm said. "And I can tell you those rocks didn't just suddenly decide to let go and pelt down on this field."

"It does happen sometimes," Hill said.

"You have rockslides like this?" Longarm demanded.

"Not just like this," Regis admitted fairly. "I've never seen this many rocks fall at one time before. But they do fall from up there, once in a while."

"Do they fall like this with a man, his legs shackled so he's damned near helpless, staked out at the foot of the cliff?"

"It could be a coincidence," Regis said.

Longarm's voice lashed out. "It would have been a hell of a coincidence if I had been killed. But I managed to break out of there. Somehow I wasn't hit, despite all they could do."

"You must not make charges you can't substantiate," Hill warned.

"Damn it, I saw somebody up there. I saw a man up there. I know you're a foot thick with your prejudices, but even you've got to admit somebody had to start those rocks tumbling down here."

"Seems reasonable, Pa," Ezekiel said hesitatingly.

Hill's head jerked up. "Did you recognize the man you saw up there?"

"No. But I know the two men who brought me and set me up here at the base of this cliff this morning—with orders to work here."

"That's what they have been instructed to do."

"You told them to bring me down here?"

"Sometimes we discuss the best places for you to start work in the morning."

"And you chose the corn rows under the cliffs this morning?"

Regis Hill looked ill, his face gray and tight. He said in a low voice, "I may have. We talked about places to start. I certainly meant you no harm."

"But you won't admit that Cutlip and Gowdy meant me harm, will you?"

"You must not make such charges—against anyone—without proof."

"My God, I've got proof that would stand up anywhere in the world except this godforsaken valley. What are you afraid of? Why won't you face them with the truth?"

Regis Hill's voice lowered, stricken. "Because, my son, we do not *know* the truth."

Longarm turned around and staggered away. He spoke over his shoulder, his voice shaking with anger. "Go to hell. Just go to hell, old man. I'll never bother to ask you for help again."

Chapter 9

From where he stood, leaning on his hoe in the Hills' beet field, Longarm watched the wagon approach along the lane.

He drew little reassurance from the rigid, stiff-backed way Elder Abel McFee rode, his Lincolnesque figure taut as if already dead set against anything Longarm might have to say. On the seat beside Abel sat Chastity and her sister, Connie.

He stood in the blazing sun, sweat leaking under the floppy straw hatbrim and running down his face. Both Chastity and Connie sat sedately, with their hands folded in their laps, as obedient and submissive Mormon women were taught to do.

Longarm shuffled between the rows of green and crimson plants in their dry hillocks. He managed to reach the side of the lane at the same time Elder McFee pulled his wagon over and looped the reins around the whipsocket on the boot.

Longarm leaned on his hoe. He looked at their faces, each in turn, finding no comfort or hope. Abel's bearded face was set. Chastity looked straight ahead. Consequence met Longarm's gaze directly, but her defiant expression said it clearly: She had done as he asked. She had brought Abel and Chastity out to talk with him. He had had no right to ask that much of

113

her. She had done for him all she could. He must know that he could not expect anything more from her.

Abel McFee swung down from the open wagon. He nodded toward Longarm, but made no move to shake hands. After a moment, Chastity stepped out of the wagon and stood beside her husband. Consequence joined her, her gaze fixed unblinkingly on Longarm's face.

Abel McFee said, "I'm sorry."

"Are you, Elder? About what?"

"All of it, Long," McFee said. "I regret now that I brought you before the Council that first day. I should only have warned you. I should have sent you on."

"Wasn't the only real question whether you were going to kill me or not?"

McFee stood straighter. "I did as I thought best at the time, and I've come to regret my decision. I'm sorry about what happened at the cliffs today, too."

"I suppose Elder Hill told you that I think Elder Waymeyer's cronies tried to kill me?"

Elder McFee exhaled heavily. "But he says you have no real proof, only suspicion.

"Must they kill me before I have the kind of evidence that will convince you people?" Longarm asked.

"They will not kill you."

"They almost killed me this morning. Can't you believe that?"

"They will not kill you, Long. They would never dare."

Longarm stared at the man's face. One of them was clearly out of touch with reality. Maybe it was he, jumpy and suspicious, seeing a threat on all sides. Or maybe it was Elder McFee, who couldn't see things the way they really were through the occluding fog of his religious prejudices. He said, "You're right about one thing, Elder McFee. They likely won't kill me unless they can make it look like an accident. But I'll still be just as dead."

"There is one question you haven't answered—for Regis Hill and his sons, and for me. Why do you think Elder Waymeyer would want you killed?"

Longarm drew a deep breath. "At first I didn't know. But I've done a lot of thinking about it, lying in that ice chest you people call a jail. I've had a feeling about Waymeyer and Cutlip and Gowdy, from the first. It's been nagging at me all along, ever since I first saw them in that meeting house. I know the Mormon people. I know them well. The Salt Lake City Mormons welcome me warmly. I've been among offshoot groups, like yours here in Alamut. I admit they haven't been as open and neighborly as those in Salt Lake City, but they tolerated me. They accepted me as a lawman who meant them no harm, who respected their rights.

"But you people are different, Elder McFee! And your so-called leader is even different from you other people. I know what that difference is."

Abel McFee sighed heavily. He did not smile, but spoke in a level, fair tone. "I will listen to you."

"They're not Mormons, Elder."

The three Mormons gasped. Their sharp intake of breath was loud in the hot stillness. They stared at Longarm. Elder McFee spoke for all of them. "How can you expect us to stand here and listen to your blasphemy?"

"Suppose it's the truth? Suppose they're Gentiles? Just like me? I say they ain't any more Mormons than I am. Wouldn't they live in fear? No matter how well they might hide it from you people? Wouldn't they be afraid someone might come in here from the outside who could expose them for what they are—and what they ain't? Wouldn't that be a good reason for killing the outsider—the stranger? Maybe they're afraid that if any stranger is allowed to leave the valley, he might tell the truth about them. And they can't afford to let that happen."

"You speak only evil, with no basis of truth to reinforce your ugly accusations," Elder McFee said.

"They came in here ten years ago, didn't they?"

"Yes, Long, they did. From the Tabernacle in Salt Lake City itself."

"Who told you they came from the Tabernacle? Did *they* tell you?"

"Yes. Of course they did."

"Did anyone else back up what they said?"

Elder McFee's face flushed. "We are not a suspicious, doubting people, Long."

"No. But you *are* simple farmers who've lived in this valley for at least two generations, cut off from the outside world. You might fall for it if a smart con man—"

Elder McFee straightened. He reached out and touched the side of his wagon. "I am sorry, Long. We must not—we cannot—stand here and listen to your baseless accusations. That is far more than you have any right to ask of us."

"All right, go ahead. Walk out on me. You're likely right. It'll only bring grief down on you if you're seen palavering with me."

"I fear no one."

"Well, you're right. I ain't got any right to say these things to you. And I'll say nothing more, Elder, if you'll just answer me one question."

Elder McFee nodded curtly.

"Have there been any other outsiders—Gentiles—murdered in the past ten years?"

Elder McFee winced. He looked down at his hands. Chastity spoke coldly. "You know there have been, Elder. You know. The Council has been outraged."

"All right," McFee said. "Elder Waymeyer and his lieutenants have been suspected in the deaths of three strangers. In each case, the deaths were investigated by the Council. In each case, we have been satisfied that Elder Waymeyer acted in what he believed to be the best interests of the people of this valley."

"But even so, the Council warned him, didn't they? They warned him that even though he's the leader in Alamut, the Council won't tolerate other murders in this community?"

"That also is true, Elder," Chastity whispered in a low, taut tone. "You have said as much to me and your other wives."

"And there have been no more murders," Elder McFee said. "We lived here in peace—until you came, Long."

"Did you?" Longarm demanded. "Did you live in peace? *Your* kind of peace? Or Elder Waymeyer's?"

"He is our leader, and loyalty is our first tenet. Our leader has the power of life and death over his followers."

"That hasn't been the way of the Mormon Church since Brigham Young, Elder! Listen to me. The Church has moved forward. The days of the Mountain Meadow Massacre, and the Mormon War, and the rigid ideas of Brigham Young, they all belong to the past. Believe me. The rules of Alamut are no longer laws of the Church in Salt Lake Valley. Salt Lake City is a big rail center now, one of the finest cities in the West. I'm telling you the gospel truth. The old rules belong to the past. You can drink a cup of coffee in Salt Lake City—in public!—without going straight to hell. Ladies wear fashions from the biggest cities, and the homes are bigger and more beautiful than some of the finest in Denver. They don't live like slaves anymore."

He stopped talking abruptly. He was aware that although Elder McFee regarded him dubiously, both Chastity and her younger sister stared at him with mouths agape. They *wanted* to believe him, whether they could or not.

Elder McFee's voice shook with agony. "Why do you come here trying to sow the seeds of discontent among my people?"

"Because they *are* your people, Elder. Yours! Not Noah Waymeyer's. He came here and passed himself off as a faithful Elder of the Golden Tabernacle. You people believed him. And he stole your rightful office from you—"

"It was the will of my people and I have accepted it."

"Still, if Waymeyer ain't even a Mormon, and I'd bet my life that he ain't, then he has as much as stolen your birthright from you. And he uses his power as spiritual leader to make himself rich—"

"Again, Gentile, your baseless accusations!" Elder McFee burst out.

"No, Elder. I can't prove yet that he *is* a Gentile, and I can't prove that he has ordered his bully boys to kill me and make it look accidental. But one thing I can prove. Waymeyer is stealing from you people. He collects outrageous tithes from your farms and businesses—and it all lines his pockets."

"We all tithe to the Church."

"This ain't just tithing. Don't take my word for it. Ask your sister-in-law, Consequence. She was in the Hills' kitchen, and so was I, when Mrs. Hill laid into Elder Hill for letting Waymeyer bleed them dry."

"If this is true, this should be brought before the Council. By Regis Hill," McFee said, "and not by you."

"Elder Hill is afraid, Mr. McFee. Maybe you know why he's scared of Waymeyer. I don't. I only know that he's scared to take a full breath. Why? Is that the way you want your people to pass their lives?"

"He does live in fear, Elder," Connie whispered.

"That's enough, Consequence." McFee made a sharp downward-cutting gesture with his hand. "I have enough to deal with, without worrying about you."

"But Consequence is one of your greatest worries." Longarm spoke passionately, staring into McFee's ashen face. "Or she should be. Consequence is loved by a young Mormon. That young fellow and Consequence might already be married—except for Elder Waymeyer."

"The Elder saw God's will in a celestial revelation," McFee said. "God wants Consequence to be Elder Waymeyer's bride."

"Are *you* sure that's God's will?"

"I do not question the celestial revelations as witnessed by my leaders," McFee raged.

"Has he had six *other* revelations?" Long asked. "He has six other wives. Do any of you others have so many?"

"He may take as many wives as he wishes, as many as he can support. That is a law of the Church."

Longarm shrugged. "It *used* to be. I say that Waymeyer steals not only your goods and money and produce, he steals your women—the best and prettiest. He takes your women, he takes your money. And what does he give you in return?"

"He gives us nothing," Chastity said in a low, firm voice.

"That's enough, Chastity!" McFee said, then turned again to Longarm. "Have you not pushed us now to the limit of our leader's patience? You have made charges, Long. You have sowed your seeds of disloyalty. For what I ask you, sir? In the name of our true God, what do you want of us?"

"I want you to take the truth to the fair-minded people of this valley—"

"Do you? I would need far more proof than you have brought me to do that. Elder Waymeyer is our leader, and our first law is our faith in our leaders, as we believe in our God—"

"*If* they deserve it."

"And even if we followed your desires, we could only take your suspicions before the Council—"

"With Elder Waymeyer at its head," Longarm said.

"That is right."

"Would they listen if I could prove he's no Mormon, no true disciple at all, but a Gentile—like me?"

"No!" The word thundered from the enraged Elder. "They would not listen. *We* will not listen. I can tell you this, Long. We may be simple, backcountry people, gullible and stupid. But I know that you do not care about our welfare—"

"That's not true. I do care."

"No. You are figuring how you can stir enough dissension among my people so that you can escape, get away from here."

"All right. I admit I want to live. Why should I die so a

118

man like Waymeyer can go on fleecing you sheep? If it's selfish to want to stay alive awhile longer, all right, I plead guilty—I'm just that selfish. But along the way, Elder, the terrible wrongs being done to your people might be paid back at the same time."

"We do not want your help, Long. We did not want you here. We do not want you stirring up trouble now."

Longarm spread his hands resignedly. "All right. That's straight enough. I'm sorry I brought you out here. I'm sorry I asked for your help. Go on back home and worship Waymeyer as you wish. I hope God will help you, because you won't help me—and if you don't help me, I can't help you."

Elder McFee jerked his head. Reluctantly, Chastity pulled herself back over the side of the wagon. She sat rigidly on the hard seat, and stared straight ahead. She looked ill. After a moment, McFee swung up beside her.

He waited, and then spoke sharply to Connie. "Are you coming with us, Consequence?"

Without taking her eyes from Longarm's face, Connie nodded. She said, in a dazed whisper, "Is that really true, Custis? All the things you say about Salt Lake City?"

He nodded wearily. "The streets ain't paved with gold, honey, but they're paved. But what do you care? Old Noah's never going to let you leave this valley. No more than he's going to let me leave it—alive."

"Come, Consequence," Chastity said in a low, quavering whisper. "You must not listen to him."

"You might as well listen to the devil himself," Abel McFee said.

Chastity seemed not to have heard her husband. She stared into the heat-shimmering distance, unseeing. "Neither of us must listen to him."

Longarm slouched against the wide-barred door of his cell. He reckoned it to be about eleven o'clock, two or three hours past nightfall. He could see not one lantern flickering across the wide expanse of the valley.

The darkness was almost impenetrable. Not even the buildings across the wide, hard-surfaced main street of the town had visible shape or form in the black night. He could barely discern the cliffs that ringed the valley, and the ranges and freedom beyond them were cut off from his vision. The dark night seemed to press in upon him like the thick walls of the dark cell.

There was no way he could reach these people. There may have been among them men of reason and fair play and common sense, but he could not find them. And without them, he was at the mercy of the spiritual tyrant of these backcountry Mormon runaways.

Longarm caught his breath involuntarily. In the stygian dark, he glimpsed movement. He gripped the bars, staring at the street.

An open wagon had pulled up at the edge of the street. After a moment someone fired up a lantern.

Holding his breath, Longarm stared as three men got down from the boot of the wagon, the lantern light bouncing oddly in the enveloping darkness.

The men did not speak. They walked unhurriedly and yet in cold determination toward the barred doors. He did not need to be told who those men were. In the vague lantern light he saw one of them spit. Noah Waymeyer. Cutlip and Gowdy sided their boss as they approached the cell.

Cutlip held the lantern. Gowdy and Waymeyer hesitated a few feet from the cell door. Cutlip walked forward, holding the lantern just above the line of his hatbrim.

Spears of the saffron light penetrated the deeper blackness of the cell.

"Long," Cutlip said. "You in there?"

"No," Longarm said. "I went into Las Vegas for a smoke."

"Stand back from that door," Cutlip ordered. "Elder Waymeyer and Gowdy and I are coming in."

Longarm backed away from the door. "Well," he said, "it's right neighborly of you to drop by."

"Just keep your mouth shut and back away from that door," Cutlip told him.

Cutlip jerked his head and Gowdy unlocked the barred door. He held it open. Cutlip walked in first, holding the lantern up so the cell was dimly lit. Waymeyer followed. Gowdy closed the door, the lock clicking loudly into place in the night silence.

Waymeyer stared at Longarm. He spat between Longarm's ragged boots and said, "We wanted to talk to you, Gentile."

Longarm shrugged. "Glad to hear a friendly voice. Talk away."

"We'll say when," Waymeyer told him. Gowdy dropped something coiled near the doorway and came toward Longarm with a snubbing length of lariat.

"Now just take it easy," Gowdy said. "We're going to tie you up a little—"

"We figure you'll listen better, and remember better," Waymeyer said. He spat on the floor again.

Longarm did not resist. He had enough trouble just staying on his feet with his legs shackled. There was no sense in going against these odds.

Gowdy worked quickly and expertly. He slipped the loop under Longarm's arms, tied his wrists, and had a six-foot tail left over. "Very neat," Longarm said. "You work as fast as an experienced bank robber."

"You shut your mouth, Gentile," Gowdy warned.

Waymeyer nodded again. Gowdy looped the end of the rope through the bars in the high window. He caught the dangling end and pulled down on it. Longarm's wrists were wrenched upward between his shoulder blades. He gasped in pain.

"Hell," Gowdy told him, "you ain't begun to hurt yet."

Gowdy tied off the rope in a tight knot, leaving Longarm hanging, bent over, his boot toes barely touching the floor.

"I think when we're through talking to you tonight," Waymeyer said, "you'll know where we stand, Gentile."

Waymeyer nodded and Gowdy took up the coiled bullwhip from the floor. Waymeyer spat and said, "Give the prisoner a couple of lashes, Gowdy. Sort of get his attention."

Gowdy stepped back. He set himself, and suddenly the bullwhip lashed out, cracking across Longarm's back. Longarm lunged and yelled, almost pulling his arms from their sockets.

"One more," Waymeyer said. "I want him to take everything I have to say to him seriously."

The whip cut across Longarm's back. The pain whipped through him like fire, the agony erupting behind his eyes, in the backs of his legs, against the top of his skull.

"You kill me, Waymeyer," Longarm said, "and you're finished here. Even you've got sense enough to know that."

"Touch him up a couple more times, Gowdy," Waymeyer said. "He's still talking. When he's ready to listen, then we'll talk."

The whip ripped at the flesh on Longarm's back.

Longarm bit down on his lip as the whip landed the second time, refusing to cry out anymore for Waymeyer and his bully boys.

Longarm tried to brace himself against the wall, his back on fire.

"What we are doing to you here tonight, Long, is only a small payment for the persecution you Gentiles have dealt out against my people—"

"You mean *us* Gentiles, Waymeyer. You're no more a Mormon than I am—" The whip sliced across his back, loud and agonizing, three more times.

Sweating, Longarm chewed at his bleeding underlip and hung at the end of the rope.

Waymeyer's quiet, level, taunting voice raked at him. "As I shall tell the Council, I was forced against my own wishes to bring the light to you, Gentile. You have been spreading dissent among my people. You have been talking against me. I shall inform the Council if this happens again—anywhere in this valley. I shall order you shot in the main street at high noon, Gentile. Do you understand me?"

Waymeyer spat again. When Longarm did not move, he came closer. "Bales here tells me you expect to be set free when your fifty days of imprisonment are ended. You misunderstood, Long. You will go free when your fine is paid off. Then and only then."

"If you live that long," Gowdy laughed.

"If you live that long," Waymeyer agreed in that low, taunting voice. "What if you had been able to force the Council to free you when your term was up, Long? I might have agreed. If there had been pressure enough, I might have agreed. I want no more trouble with these people than necessary. Do you really think that would have ensured your safe passage out of here?" He spat on the floor, laughed, and shook his head. "I'm surprised at how stupid you are, Long. If I were forced to release you, I would do it. I would let you go. I would let you leave this valley. But think, Long. Think. It's a long way across the desert to the railhead at Las Vegas. A very long way for an unarmed man." He spat again. "Do you really think you'd make it alive, Long?"

Longarm hung there, silent.

Waymeyer grabbed Longarm's hair in his hand and jerked his head up, then released him and turned away. "Cut the son of a bitch down now, Gowdy. I think he's begun to see what kind of spot he's in."

Gowdy released the rope, leaving Longarm's wrists bound. Longarm plunged forward on his face, only inches from a glob of brown spittle on the floor.

He lay unmoving. Waymeyer and his boys stood over him for a few silent moments. Then the heavy door was opened and they walked out. The lantern was doused, and the cell was plunged again into blackness.

The iron bars clanged shut. Longarm stayed where he was, swimming in a hot pool of pain.

He heard the slap of reins, the creak of leather and metal, as the open wagon moved away in the darkness. He took a painful breath and inhaled the sharp, acrid odor of tobacco. Chewing tobacco.

His heart beat faster. Though he lay tied, helpless and bleeding, he felt his first real surge of hope. Waymeyer had made a serious mistake. He had thought he would intimidate Longarm, as he had frightened Regis Hill and the others, but he had not only failed, he had provided Longarm the proof he needed not only to stop Waymeyer, but to nail his crooked hide to the wall.

He grinned in the darkness, and then he smiled, and then laughter grew and burst from him.

He was still alive. He still had one more chance at freedom, a chance provided by the self-styled Elder himself.

Chapter 10

Longarm lay swollen and bleeding, his face pressed against the floor, when Cutlip and Gowdy returned at daybreak.

"Holy mother," Gowdy said. "What a mess."

Bales Cutlip laughed. "Yeah. Looks like he had quite a party in here last night."

Gowdy brought in a bucket of water from the town well and doused it on Longarm. He sat up slowly, feeling the pain ebbing slightly.

He even managed to grin at Waymeyer's bully boys. "Had a hell of a dream last night. Dreamt you fellows dropped by to see me. Yeah. And not only you, but the head rooster of this whole valley. He's a real Mormon son of a bitch, ain't he? Spittin' tobacco juice all over the place."

Cutlip backhanded him across the face. "Keep your mouth shut, Gentile, or what you got last night will seem like nothing."

Longarm grinned coldly at him. "Just remember, Bales, I'm keeping score."

Bales Cutlip looked as if he might kick Longarm in the face, but managed to get his mindless rage under control. He jerked his head, ordering Gowdy to loosen the ropes at Longarm's

125

wrists and about his chest. "Let's get him the hell out of here. He'll feel great after a few hours in the sun."

Longarm got up slowly, awkwardly. He staggered toward the open door and hesitated a moment, leaning against its jamb. He twisted his battered face into a grim smile. "I'm still a hell of a lot better off than you two bastards, Cutlip. I'm going to get well, and you're not."

Old Regis Hill stared at Longarm, shocked.

Longarm lay in the farmyard where Gowdy had thrown him out before Cutlip yanked the wagon around and headed back toward Alamut.

Connie and the Hill family came running out onto the porch. Connie screamed. Ned and Zeke came down the steps, lifted him up, and helped him into the shade of the rear porch.

He sank into a cane-bottomed chair and stretched his legs before him. Connie's eyes were brimming with tears, but she said nothing.

Clara Hill stood gripping her apron in both hands, staring at him.

"My God," Elder Hill whispered. "What happened to you?"

Longarm didn't look up at him. "What do you care, old man? I had a bad night. Got worked over by three of your stalwart citizens. But I won't try to tell you who they were. There was nothing but lantern light, and as you like to say, I don't have proof."

"I'm sorry," Hill whispered. "Before God, I am sorry."

"The hell with it." Longarm's voice rasped at him. "I've been hurt before in the line of duty. If I live to get out of this paradise, I'll likely get hurt again."

"You poor man," Clara Hill said.

Still, Longarm didn't look up. "Don't fret yourself, ma'am." He sighed. "You're a good woman. You tried to tell them, but they won't listen to you and they won't listen to me—"

"You ask too much of us," Regis Hill said. "Too much. Would you have me killed? And my sons? Do you want us to lose this farm? Will that help you?"

"I don't want anything from you, old man. I just thought you might want to look at me. See my legs? They're shackled together. I can't take a full step. I fall down a lot. That makes me kind of helpless. And when you're helpless enough, you become the prey of cowardly men who wouldn't dare face you if you were strong."

Hill spread his hands. "Do you want me to admit my weakness? I admit it to you."

"You're wrong. You keep talking about what I ask of you. I don't ask anything of you. Nothing. As soon as I get my hoe, I'll get out in the beet fields. As soon as I'm out of your sight, I'll be out of your mind."

"You make us sound evil, Long," Hill said. "We are not evil."

"I didn't say evil, Elder Hill. Maybe you don't listen good. I said weak. And they know you are weak. They prey on the weak. And you're probably next. That's all I said."

"I must live," Hill whispered. "I must protect my family as best I can."

"You do that. You go on protecting them as you are. And God help you. Now if you people will just go back in the house, I'll get on out to the beet fields."

"You can't work in this condition," Hill said.

"The hell I can't. I will work. By God, I'll work out there until I drop. They're going to kill me, sure they are. But they're going to *have to* kill me. I won't ask pity from them, any more than I'll ask it of you. I want nothing from you, nothing from them. They can kill me, Elder Hill. But there's one thing they can't do to me that they *can* do to the rest of you people. They can't make me get on my knees to them and beg."

Elder Hill pressed the back of his huge fist against his whiskered mouth. "We are weak, Long. And afraid. Is that what you want to know? But you knew that all along, didn't you?"

"No." Longarm shook his head and stared at the ground. "For a little while I thought maybe you and your sons had the grit your wife has got. Now I know better. I don't give a damn. What happens to you from now on is up to you. I won't get in your way again. And I won't ask for your help again."

Longarm pulled himself to his feet, braced himself as well as he could with his legs apart, and almost fell. Connie leaped to grab his arm and support him.

He shook free. "Don't get mixed up in this," he told her.

"Please, Custis," she whispered. "Don't treat me like this."

He stepped toward the support at the edge of the steps, and

gripped it and hung on while the world spun about his head.

"Isn't there anything we can do for you?" Hill begged.

"Yeah. Why not? Why leave you anything? I'm going to tell you the truth. And it's going to scare the living hell out of you. But you're going to have to live with it. That's the price of getting mixed up with me. But I'm not telling you this truth just to punish you or put you in danger. You asked what you could do for me. Well, I'll tell you. You can tell any fair-minded man in this valley—if you can find one—you can tell him that the Gentile finally has the hard evidence that your beloved Elder Waymeyer isn't an Elder. Hell, he ain't even a Mormon."

"Oh, my God. Haven't they done enough to you? Must you go on fighting them?"

"Yes. I've already told you yes. I'll fight the bastards until they kill me. I won't get on my knees and close my eyes and let them steal me blind. I know, I'm too tough on you, Hill. I know you're gut-scared of Waymeyer. Scared until you can't sleep at night. I don't know why. I don't care why. You've got to live with your fear, I don't. Hell, maybe it's as simple as being afraid the head Elder will take this place from you."

Hill stared at him, pleading. Then the words rushed out, words that had to be said before he lost the courage to speak them aloud, even here in his own home.

"I—have been warned, Long. I—I did oppose Elder Waymeyer once, when he took his fourth wife. Magdalena was his fourth wife. She was my only daughter. Seventeen years old when he took her after a revelation. I fought against him. I was condemned before the Council. Elder Waymeyer said he would treat me with mercy. He would show compassion. He would let me return here—my family and I could work this place—until I defied him again. If I dared oppose him again, he warned me he would denounce me before the Council and strip me of my worldly possessions."

Longarm exhaled heavily. "All right, forget it. I have been too tough on you and your sons. I have asked too much of you. I ask no more."

He moved to go down the steps. But Hill touched his arm. "You said you had proof. We want to hear it."

"We want to hear it, Mr. Long," Clara Hill said.

"It can't help you any. It can only hurt you." Longarm shook his head.

"The fear we live in," Elder Hill said. "It could be no worse. If you know the truth, let us at least share that burden with you."

Longarm stood there a long time, silent. At last he spoke in a low tone. "All right. Most of this you know. Waymeyer sends wagons once a month. Fresh truck and corn are sold by Waymeyer's henchmen in Las Vegas. And they pick up supplies. And he takes a tenth of your goods for tithing."

"He takes a third," Clara Hill said. "But we all know this. We also know the Church takes only a tenth at Salt Lake."

"Tithing *is* a tenth." Longarm shrugged. "But it's some of the supplies Elder Waymeyer buys that have proved to me he ain't a Mormon, any more than I am. I know, and every one of you people in this valley knows, no Mormon smokes. So there ain't any tobacco grown in this valley, is there?"

"Of course not," Hill said.

"And yet Waymeyer keeps a cud of it in his mouth. You settlers, raised here in the valley, have never seen a tobacco leaf in your lives. You wouldn't know one if you saw it. You'd all know a man was using tobacco if he smoked it, but you people who have never been around tobacco—haven't you ever wondered why old Noah spits so much?"

"Tobacco," Zeke Hill whispered.

"Tobacco." Elder Hill shook his head.

"Why would an hombre pretending to be a good Mormon, a Mormon Elder from the Tabernacle at Salt Lake City, be dumb enough to use tobacco and jeopardize his personal gold mine?" Longarm grinned ruefully. "It may be hard for you to understand. Maybe you *can't* understand it. But I can. Waymeyer had to give up all his other luxuries and vices when he came here as your Elder. But he couldn't give up tobacco. I think about the way I want a cheroot sometimes, and I know what he went through. I know how hard it is to break all those filthy little habits. So Noah found he could chew tobacco— and spit—and you farmers would never think a thing about it. He's probably got some other revealing Gentile habits—and I'd be willing to bet there are wanted fliers out on him—or were, ten years ago. You're right—I can't prove that. Not yet. But I do know what chewing tobacco looks like, what it tastes like and smells like, and the way it makes a man spit."

* * *

The rest of the day passed in taut silence on the Hill farm. The sun blazed down, and sweat burned the cuts across Longarm's back. The heat seemed to boil up from the brown dust of the valley floor. The sky was bleached by the sun. Longarm spent most of the day leaning on the hoe.

He had one satisfaction. The truth was at large in Alamut Valley. It could not be recalled. It could not be beaten to its knees. Waymeyer and his plug-uglies couldn't kill everybody who would soon hear the horrified whisper. It was as if the truth rode on the wind across the valley.

Still, he remained beaten, cut, and battered—and shackled. Waymeyer couldn't kill all his followers, but once the tobacco story got back to him, the order would surely go out: Kill Long first and then figure some way to deny the story.

It was late afternoon, almost time for supper, when he saw his ticket to freedom approaching the farm along the road from town.

He called to Connie. She came out to the rear porch, where he sat alone.

"Martin Haswell is coming to see you," he said. "If you want to keep from being forced into marrying Elder Waymeyer, if you'd like to see the streets and dresses and houses in Salt Lake City, you've got one chance."

She bit her lip. "I'll do anything you tell me, Custis."

He nodded. "All right. You go out to the barn, and stay there until I come out there—or call you. Will you do that?"

They watched the approaching wagon and the big-shouldered young blacksmith holding the reins. Martin wore his best suit; he was freshly bathed and shaved. She nodded.

Longarm watched Connie walk across the yard, her lithe figure and flaxen hair. When she was inside the barn, Longarm slowly descended the steps. He stood out in the yard when Martin drove his wagon to a hitching rack and halted his horse. The man was grinning, but he was already looking around for Connie.

Longarm said, "I waited out here for you, Haswell."

"Yeah?" Haswell swung down from the wagon. He tried to be polite, but his eyes were moving constantly, searching for Consequence Knight.

"Elder Hill wants you to check the shoes on his best horse. He don't want you to do anything but just look at them. If there is something wrong, why, you can take the mare back to town with you tonight and fix it tomorrow at the blacksmith shop. He just wants you to check it."

Reluctantly, Haswell agreed. "I hate to mess up these good clothes."

"Don't have to touch the horse," Longarm promised. "I do the lifting, you just check."

They entered the barn. For a moment they blinked against the darkness of the hay-smelling interior. Then Connie came out of one of the stalls.

Haswell smiled, grinned, shook his head. "What you doing out here, Consequence?"

Connie glanced toward Longarm. "I was waiting for you, Martin. Mr. Long has something to tell you."

Puzzled, Haswell glanced toward Longarm. He was already shaking his head. "I don't listen to no talk against the Elders, Mr. Long. Everybody knows we all must follow the instructions of our Elders. Anything else is a sin."

"You don't think it's a sin to give up Connie—to an old man, maybe as old as I am?"

He saw Connie restrain a faint smile, but he ignored her, watching the young blacksmith's simple, handsome face. "Do you want Elder Waymeyer—or anybody else—to have that girl? Look at her. Connie is the loveliest girl in this valley. But you're going to let Elder Waymeyer take her from you."

"There's nothing else I can do."

"You could take her away from here," Longarm persisted. "Now. Tonight."

"How could I do that? Where would I take her? What would we live on?"

"You're an expert blacksmith, Martin. You could be a blacksmith anywhere. Even in Salt Lake City."

"I'd like that, Martin," Connie said.

Haswell stared at his love, anguished. "Now you are siding with him. You are talking like he talks—the talk of the devil."

"Is it the talk of the devil to want Connie bad enough to fight for her? Are you going to be able to stay in this valley, knowing every night that he's making Connie lie down with him in his bed—probably with another of his seven wives on the other side of him?"

Haswell looked gray. "You must not talk like this," he whispered. He stood with his fists clenched at his sides.

"I'm talking the truth, Martin. Once Elder Waymeyer takes

Connie as his wife, it's too late. You have lost her. But you could run with her—tonight—if you're willing to fight for her. You got this one chance. You agree to help me get free—and I'll help you and Connie get to Las Vegas, and put you on a train to Salt Lake City. She'll be all yours, the way God must have meant it."

Haswell shook his head. "I don't know. I never went against the Elders."

"It's your one chance, Martin. If they kill me, I can't help you get Connie away from here. And you won't be able to do it against Noah Waymeyer. You've got to make up your mind."

"I don't know," Haswell muttered, confused. "I don't know."

"You better find out," Longarm said. "And in a hurry. I'm going to leave you here in this barn with Consequence, Martin. Don't worry about the Hills. I'll lie to them about where you are. You better sit and talk with Consequence and make up your mind once and for all if you're willing for Waymeyer to take her from you, to use, to bed down, to—"

"Stop it," Martin growled.

"Please stay, Martin," Connie whispered. "I want you to."

"Listen to her, Martin," Longarm said. "Consequence will love you—she will love you because you alone can arouse her true emotions—"

"I'll do all I know," Connie whispered.

Inwardly, Longarm grinned. Connie was working for him now. And no matter how straitlaced and religious Martin Haswell was, he didn't have a chance against her wiles. Longarm knew this, even as he felt a twist in his own loins with the knowledge that he would never have her again.

Longarm shuffled away toward the big front doors of the barn. Behind him he heard Connie whispering to Martin, drawing him with her into one of the hay-filled stalls. He heard Martin protesting, and heard those protests ebb and die.

He hesitated at the door and glanced back. They were no longer in sight. Connie had drawn Martin after her into one of those beds of hay. In a few moments, when that dress went up, Martin's whole world was going to turn upside down.

Longarm drew a deep breath and exhaled heavily. Well, there was nothing more he could do now. It was in the hands of the gods—and in the hands and mouth and thighs of Consequence Knight.

He found the Hills considerate and incurious about where Consequence Knight and Martin Haswell had gotten to. Then he realized that though the Gentiles found the Mormons rigid on stimulants and tobacco and alcohol, the Disciples were much more forbearing in their attitude toward sex.

He was glad for this. Time sped past, and there was no sign of Martin or Connie returning from the barn.

Longarm felt his heart sink. Tonight was his only chance to escape this valley alive. If Connie could not convince Martin to go against his religious training, he was lost.

Zeke brought the wagon around. "Might as well drive you into town, Mr. Long," he said.

"I reckon." Longarm stood up slowly in the shadows and walked toward the wagon.

Ned was helping Longarm up into the rear of the wagon when the barn door was pushed open.

Longarm felt a surge of triumph. Haswell staggered out through the door, his clothing twisted and full of hay, his hair mussed and wild. His eyes seemed glazed, as if he had looked on incredible beauty he still could not believe.

He called out, "Mr. Long, could I talk to you for one moment?"

Chewing at the smile that tugged at his mouth, Longarm nodded. He was thankful that the gathering shadows and the floppy brim of his straw hat concealed most of his face. "I've got something I want to say to you, Mr. Long." Martin's voice sounded odd, stunned.

Longarm shuffled to where Martin stood. "All right, Martin, what is it?" he said.

Martin stared at him in the gathering dark. "I won't let him have her, Mr. Long. I won't let anybody have her. I can't live without her, Mr. Long. I know that now. No matter what happens, I am going to keep her."

"If you want her, Martin, you're going to have to fight for her."

Chapter 11

Longarm figured it was around midnight when he heard a whisper of sound beyond the doors of his cell. He moved back against the wall and waited with his hands at his sides. After a moment, in the unbroken darkness of the town, he could make out the crouched form of something that looked like a grizzly bear and moved with the stealth of an Apache. Longarm grinned, his heart leaping. "Haswell," he whispered.

He watched the man bent over at the door in the darkness, and shuffled slowly across the room. This was the first he had heard from the young blacksmith since they had parted in Regis Hill's backyard at dusk. He had waited and hoped, and waited more and despaired.

The looming figure went on working swiftly. Longarm could tell in the deep blackness that Haswell had put a piece of cloth over the deadbolt lock. "It's me, Long." There was no warmth in the blacksmith's voice, but there was the hint of terror and the agony of guilt. After all, Connie and Longarm were asking him to go against his religion and that of his forefathers. It was not a decision a man made easily. "I still ain't sure I'm doing the right thing."

"Trust me," Longarm said. "You're doing the *only* thing you can do."

"I never went against God before in my life."

"Do you really believe God wants you to live out the rest of your life on this earth without Connie?"

"All right. All right. I'm here. I just hope you know more about what God wants than I do."

"I don't know what God wants. Nobody does. But do you know what I believe He wants? He wants us poor mortals to find whatever happiness we can while we're here. I don't believe it's all that dead serious. I believe we can enjoy the good things God has put on this earth, and still stay in good with Him."

The young blacksmith exhaled heavily, and Longarm saw Haswell kneel, raise a heavy hammer in his right fist, and bring it down on a cloth-covered chisel held in his left.

Longarm marveled at the strength and expertise of the youth. The door swung open easily. There had been only the slightest sound, no more than a fist against a pillow, a faint noise lost in the midnight breezes.

Breathing uneasily, Martin stepped inside the cell. He brought the cloths, hammer, chisel, and a wooden block. He set up the block. "Put your leg so the shackle is on the edge of the block. It might hurt a little—"

"Never has a little hurt promised such sweet pleasure," Longarm said.

Martin grunted and placed a piece of cloth between Longarm's ankle and the metal. "I've known dentists less careful than you," Longarm said. "In fact, I never knew a dentist as careful as you."

Martin said nothing. He grasped the cloth-matted chisel again and struck it once, sharply, with the hammer. The metal parted and fell to the cell floor with a clank, the loudest sound Haswell had made so far. "And now I'm as guilty as you," the blacksmith whispered.

"It's going to be worth it, Martin," Longarm said.

Martin grunted again and placed the other shackle on the battered block. "I reckon if I was wearing these shackles, I'd promise anything to get out of them," he said.

Longarm grinned and spread his hands. "Then we understand each other. I'll tell you the truth, Martin. I can't wait for my left leg to feel as free as my right one."

Haswell struck with the hammer, and the shackles and chain fell away. He stood up, stocky and broad-shouldered and miserable. He threw the hammer aside. "We best get out of here."

Longarm was massaging his ankles. He straightened, nodding. "Ain't you going to take your things with you?"

"Why?" The youth asked. "Do you think there's going to be any mystery about who helped you escape?"

"Where is Connie?"

Haswell seemed far from convinced that the path he followed led to salvation. "I left her at the blacksmith shop. No sense mixing her up in this, in case I was caught over here."

"You'll live a long time in heaven, Martin," Longarm said. "You deserve it because you're a good man."

Haswell led the way out of the cell. "I don't know why you remind me of a man selling snake oil off the back of a wagon."

Longarm grinned. "You've got to have more faith, Martin. It's a long way to Las Vegas."

"Never mind Las Vegas, snake-oil man, let's just get out of here for right now."

Consequence was huddled in the darkness of the blacksmith shop. As they approached in the darkness, Haswell whispered her name. She leaped up from the shadows and ran to them. But instead of going to Martin, she caught Longarm's biceps in both hands. "Are you all right?"

"Martin's the man did all the work," Longarm said pointedly.

Connie smiled. She reached out and smoothed Martin's arm. "Martin and I will be together for a long time."

"Not unless we get out of here," Martin said. "There's one wagon road through the pass in the cliffs. It's wide enough for a cart or coach. And it's sure to be guarded. That means we've got to go out over a goat path I know. Found it when I was a kid. Most men—and girls—around here know it. But it's not guarded."

"That means we can't take horses," Longarm said under his breath.

"That's right. That's why I believe you've sold Connie a crate of snake oil."

"We'll make it, Martin," Consequence said with savage intensity. "We'll make it to Las Vegas and we'll make it to Salt Lake City. Won't we, Custis?"

"I'd bet my life on it," Longarm said, but he no longer spoke with the same assurance as when he'd believed they'd be riding horses.

"Sure you would, snake-oil man," Martin said. "That's fair enough. And you'd stake my life. And that's fair enough. If Connie marries Elder Waymeyer, I might as well be dead. But you're staking Connie's life too, and—"

"And that's fair," Connie said. "We'll make it. I know we will. I don't say it will be easy. But I'll try to be worth it to you, Martin. I swear I will."

Martin almost smiled in the darkness. "Let's get started," he said.

Consequence had brought a Hawken rifle from the Hills' farm. Haswell supplied two rifles, two aged handguns, and two well-oiled leather gunbelts with ammunition. They carried only the barest essentials, along with the weapons in pouches lashed across a burro's back. As Connie and Martin prepared the pack animal, Longarm filled six canteens with cold, sweet water from the town well.

They walked away from the rear of the blacksmith shop, leading the burro, and headed north.

"Las Vegas is west," Longarm pointed out.

"You should have told the goats where to make their path," Martin said. "They wanted to go north."

Longarm paused, staring toward the distant palisades of sandstone, looming like dark parapets to the north. It was a long way across the cultivated valley to the goat path that would lead them out of the Mormon community. A light sleeper, a barking dog, or a braying of their burro would betray them.

He said, "Maybe you're right, Martin. Maybe you and Connie ought to stay here."

"Sure," Martin said. "I can take your place in jail when Elder Waymeyer finds you're gone and I freed you."

"And I can marry Elder Waymeyer. I'd rather be dead, Custis," Connie said. "You know that. I could never marry a man that old."

"You're right," Longarm said. "He's damned near my age."

Connie laughed faintly in the darkness. "Old is different in different people, Custis."

"Well, you just try to keep Martin young," Longarm said in a firm tone.

"Then let's stop talking and make tracks out of here," Connie said.

Longarm grinned, but there were things that had to be said, and before they reached the distant goat path in the north cliffs.

"Maybe my best move would be to get to Las Vegas alone, and get some backing—Utah Territorial Police, deputy marshals."

"No, Custis," Connie said. "We're going with you. By the time you got back here, no matter who you brought, it'd all be over for Martin and me."

"They'll be after us soon after daybreak," Longarm told her. "You've got to look at the odds. There's a lot more of them than there is of us. Maybe it'd be better to stay here and try to rouse as many of the people as we can against Waymeyer."

"You're talking about a shooting war," Haswell said. "We wouldn't have a chance. Most of the people would back the Council of Elders, and they'd back Elder Waymeyer for sure. The whole valley'd rise up against us."

"I reckon so," Longarm agreed. "We're between a rock and a hard place, that's for sure. Well, we'd best get a move on. At sunrise they'll be after us on horses, and I'd just as soon they didn't catch us still in the valley. Strikes me that the best place to be would be that goat path—at least they won't be able to surround us. You go along with that, Martin?"

The blacksmith shrugged. "It's impossible any other way."

"Fair enough," Longarm said. "That's the decision. Let's go—and no looking back."

Haswell laughed ironically. "Maybe you misunderstood me, Long," he said. "I said it was impossible any other way. I didn't say it was possible this way."

They were almost running when they reached the base of the cliffs. Martin found the faint trace of the trail at the foot of the slope. He glanced back once across the dark valley, and said, "You and Connie go ahead, Long. Connie has been up this trail before. You follow her. I'll drag the burro. I know how to handle him. When you get out on the other side, keep going, and I'll catch up with you."

With Connie, wearing Levi's and a corduroy jacket and an old straw hat, moving ahead of him, Longarm struggled up the goat path. He was soon breathing raggedly, and his legs felt weak from climbing after the long days of shuffling in half-steps on flat ground.

She soon found the trail, which carried them upward across a short rise, and then along a rocky ledge. Misshapen hulks of rocks reared up around them, their surfaces sand-pitted and time-smoothed. She stumbled in the darkness and fell back against him. He caught her, his hands inadvertently closing on her full breasts. He heard her gasp in the darkness. But Martin was fighting a burro up this impossible path behind them. Longarm released her quickly, set her on her feet, and slapped her bottom, sending her forward.

"I'll miss you, Custis," she whispered over her shoulder.

"Not unless we get out of this alive, you won't. Keep climbing. Don't talk so much. Save your breath."

They could hear Martin cursing the burro on the backtrail. He was finding it slow going, leading the jackass through the rocks and along the high ledges.

They reached the crest of the high fault and started on the down trail. The path was narrow; they forced their way between the rock ledges and the sharp shafts of flint.

Connie stumbled and went spilling along the trail. Supporting himself on the knifelike walls, Longarm hurried after her. By the time he reached her, on the rim of a ledge, she was brushing off her Levi's.

"Are you all right?" he said.

"Nothing is going to keep me away from Las Vegas," she said. But from then on, she moved more cautiously.

They came down the slope on the north side of the ridge. In the faint moonlit darkness, there lay only a vast expanse of sage-matted wasteland.

"We better wait," Longarm said.

"He told us to go on."

"Sure. But we're going to head west—or what I think is west. He and I may not have the same sense of direction."

She slumped down with her back against a rock. After what seemed an eternity in the darkness, they heard Martin swearing at the burro.

Martin came at a run off the narrow trail. He stopped, stunned with shock to find them waiting for him. "You could have been a mile out there by now," he said.

"We waited," Connie said.

"It's a long way," Longarm said. "I figured we'd do better traveling together. It's about twenty miles to Las Vegas, right?"

"Twenty miles of desert," Martin agreed.

"I figure ten or twelve hours at best," Longarm said. "There may be times in the heat when we can't travel at all."

Dawn, and then bright daylight, streaked about them in what seemed an eternally widening expanse of emptiness. The sun, directly behind them, crawled like some fearsome serpent from behind broken ridges. With daybreak, a constant wind, rising from the pits beyond hell, stung their faces and sprayed fine alkali granules into their eyes.

Connie stopped often for water.

Longarm said, "I figure two canteens before noon—we ought to make it on the other three."

"Let her have all she wants," Martin said. "I'm not thirsty."

"You will be," Longarm told him.

"I don't think so," Martin said, tugging on the burro's rope. "I'm too scared to be thirsty. By now they know you're gone. Soon they'll know we're gone too. They might have let us go, except Elder Waymeyer is not going to let Connie get away from him if he can stop her."

"That dirty old man," Connie said, stopping again for water.

Martin paused about an hour later. The sun blazed behind them now, as if it too were pursuing them. They surveyed the desolate expanse of saline flats and scrub-crusted plains, all stretching north and south like huge, elongated lakes from another age. Ahead of them in the blue distance, Martin recognized a peak. He had no idea how far away it was, but he figured that by keeping it as a goal, they were bound to pass somewhere close to Las Vegas. Somewhere among the sage and faults and flats, they would find the settlement. "We could miss the settlement, though," he said. "There's not much there."

"We'll look for the railroad tracks," Longarm said. "They follow the north-south basins, crossing them. We find the tracks, we'll find the settlement."

Longarm tried to stare across the space toward that peak, gray in the distance, but the glare off the sand was blinding him already, and it was only the shank of the morning. He pulled his hat down to cut some of the glare and to keep out the blast of wind-driven sand.

They found few signs that anyone had ever crossed this godforsaken basin. He plodded with his head down. Walking across blazing and barren wastes reminded him of the feat of those early Mormons—Martin's grandparents—and what they had accomplished. He felt a new respect for their achievement in making a flowering place in this desert.

Longarm extended his first estimates from twelve hours to fourteen, or maybe even twenty, as the time it would take them to reach Las Vegas. This arid, broken land looked flat, but it was hard to walk on, and heat rose from it, dry and stifling. They crossed rocky, treacherous places with the petrified skeletons of miniature junipers like dried bones in the sun. Flat-topped mesas loomed ahead of them, and keeping the tip of the distant peak in view, they wasted precious time going around the high, rearing faults.

Martin pointed out buzzards circling overhead. "They got their eyes on us," he said in sour levity.

"If they want me, they'll have to come to Salt Lake City," Connie said, but her voice sounded strained, and weakening. The buzzards kept passing between them and the sun, casting ragged, fleeting shadows over them.

They kept walking, heads down, the sun basting them mercilessly in their own sweat. The wind burned Longarm's cheeks and the sand blinded him. His eyes watered. It hurt when he blinked; his eyelids were charred and grainy.

He glanced back. The burro was holding up well enough so far, and moved willingly with Martin's hand on its lead rope. But he was afraid even the courageous little animal would finally give out under the relentless sun. He saw that Connie no longer led the way. She walked beside the burro, sometimes bracing her hand against the pouches to support herself.

He looked about for a single tree that might afford a few feet of shade, and found none. They needed to rest, but sitting in this open sun would buy them nothing except sunstroke.

They crested a sage-clotted knoll, and Longarm caught sight of a twisted pinyon, with two arms like tiny sun parasols. The tree grew out of rocks on the crest of a low ridge. "Is it worth climbing up there for shade?" he said to Martin, pointing toward the pinyon.

"Yeah. We could hang the pouches on those limbs. That would add a little shade. We all need the rest," Martin said.

They plodded upward, cresting two lesser ridges that they had not even noticed in staring at the pinyon, which had looked so inviting and so near. It was neither. The ground was slashed and strewn with rocks and boulders. But there was the promise of a few square inches of shade, and they fought upward toward it.

They climbed, panting, sun-blistered, for an eternity. The sun climbed with them, burning them relentlessly. The glare intensified until it was almost blinding.

When Connie staggered in the rocks for the third time, Longarm went back to her. He swung her up in his arms and stumbled across the broken ridges to the shadows.

He set her down in the widest spread of shade. She sprawled out, gasping for breath. Martin reached them. He hung up the leather pouches. They pulled down the limbs, but added a few inches of shade. They hugged it. Martin brought a canteen of water.

He spoke to Connie, but she did not answer. She was staring off along their backtrail. Both Martin and Longarm stood, gazing from the ridge toward distant puffs of dust.

"Oh, Custis," she said. "Martin. Look. It's them."

Neither Martin nor Longarm bothered to contradict her. For some moments they squinted through the white glare of sun. "I count three," Longarm said.

"That's right," Martin agreed. "And they're moving pretty fast in this heat."

As they watched, the riders, formless images in the shimmering heat, broke the rhythm of their pace. They walked their horses, and then speeded them, trotting.

"We better get moving," Martin said. "They'll run us down if we don't."

Longarm nodded. What he was thinking he did not put into words. The riders would run them down anyway. The shadows of the circling buzzards flashed across them. Sometimes those vultures seemed to know more than a man did. They were up higher, maybe they could see further. Maybe the sun didn't blur their vision. Maybe they didn't let false hope interfere with plain logic.

"It's Elder Waymeyer," Connie said. "I know it is."

"Figures," Longarm said. He glanced back across the wastes. Those forms were oddly silhouetted against blue heat waves. But Longarm was sure he could name them. He extended his hand to help Connie to her feet as Martin returned the pouches to the burro's back.

Connie started to get up, gasped, and fell back. She couldn't make it. Stunned, Longarm stared at her right boot. Her ankle was swollen against the leather. "I sprained it," she whispered. "I'm afraid I sprained it, back when I fell—on that goat path."

Chapter 12

Longarm stood in the rocks and watched the riders approach through the sea of sage and the shimmer of heat. The sun seemed to explode, unbearable and unceasing. Sweat coursed along his salt- and sand-streaked face.

Beside him, Connie sprawled in agony. Her face was bloodless, and she kept biting at her mouth to keep from screaming aloud.

Martin, watching the three riders below them, but more troubled about Connie, knelt beside her. "I better get that boot off her," he said.

Without taking his gaze from the pursuing riders, Longarm spoke over his shoulder. "If you do, you'll never get it back on her."

"She can't walk anyway," Martin said.

"The boot will protect her foot and leg. Pour cold water down in her boot. If we get out of this, we'll put her on the burro and tote the pouches. If we don't get out of it, it won't matter anyway. Waymeyer will take her back on the horses."

Martin sighed and poured water down her boot. It was almost as if they could hear the water sizzle against her flesh. Martin's face twisted with concern.

"It feels better, Martin," Connie said, to reassure him. "I'll be all right."

Longarm watched the riders. The shimmering heat made it nearly impossible to figure distances, but those men seemed less than a mile away.

Through the haze, Longarm watched the riders pause, check for sign in the sage, find it, and race forward again. For what seemed an eternity, he stood unmoving. They appeared enormously and grotesquely large and misshapen in the blinding sunlight. Noah Waymeyer rode point, a kerchief across his nose, his hatbrim pulled down against the sand and wind. Cutlip and Gowdy sided the false Elder, armed and alert. Longarm heard their horses' hooves crack and slash at the crisp alkali earth.

"God help us," Martin whispered. "They've caught us."

"They haven't got us yet," Longarm said.

"I want a gun," Connie said.

"You stay down there where you are," Longarm said.

"I don't know about you," she said. "But I don't mean to let those men near me without a fight."

"We'll fight," Longarm agreed. "Because we've got to. There's nothing else we can do."

"Thank God there's only three of them," Martin said. "That's better odds than we could have hoped for. They could have brought some of the people with them."

"They didn't want to," Longarm told him. "That's because they knew who we were, and where we were headed. They mean to stop us, and take Connie back alive. They didn't want any Mormon witnesses to what they plan to do to you and me."

Silently, Martin broke out rifles from the pouches. He gave one to Connie, who sat with the weapon across her lap.

Longarm took a rifle, loaded it, and held it in his fist at his side. He said, "We're kind of sitting with our backs to the wall. But damn few of these rocks are big enough to offer any protection." He glanced toward the circling buzzards. "We ain't got much time left to decide what we're going to do."

"We're going to stay and fight," Connie said. "I can't move."

"We could put you on the burro, tie you on, and keep moving. They'd have to ride in on us. Our chances of stopping them are exactly as good as theirs of staying alive to take us."

Martin watched the riders, then glanced at Connie. "Connie

is pretty well protected in there," he said. "Why don't we leave her there? You take whatever cover you can find in these rocks."

"And you?" Longarm said.

"I'll lead the burro down the slope and out onto the flats. They're still far enough away so that maybe, in this heat, they won't be sure I'm alone. They may follow me. If they follow just long enough so that we get them in between us, we'll be in better shape than we are like this."

Longarm nodded. "Good point. They're mighty close right now. You better get going. And Martin?"

"Yeah, Snake-oil man?"

"Good luck."

Longarm wasted only time enough to see Martin take up the lead rope and move swiftly downslope.

He jerked his head around, and found the riders looming larger than ever in the shimmering sunlight; they were following the burro's tracks up the lower slopes toward the solitary pinyon. The shadows of the vultures had shrunk; the birds had wisely caught an updraft to carry them out of harm's way. If the buzzards could smell death, it made sense that they could also smell danger in the desert.

"Get into the rocks, Custis," Connie said.

He turned and glanced at her. "Oh, shit," he said.

"What's the matter, Custis?"

"You. You're out of the direct sun pretty good, and you got a boulder at your back, but no protection otherwise. You could be hit by stray bullets. Old Noah won't mind leaving Martin and me for the buzzards, but if he accidentally killed you, he'd be sick for the rest of the day."

"I'm all right," she insisted.

"The hell you are. This boulder beside you"—he caught it and strained—"I'm going to pull it down against these rocks and you'll be in a little cubbyhole. It ain't perfect, but it will help."

He strained, pulling on the boulder, and felt it move. He kept working until its dark side rolled up to the sun and it stopped, braced against smaller rocks.

He turned to glance back toward the riders when Connie's faint, terrorized voice stopped him. "Custis. Oh, my God, Custis!"

He heeled around and stopped, frozen in his tracks.

Connie crouched behind the boulders, staring wide-eyed and frozen at something in the spot from which Longarm had moved the boulder.

He didn't blame her. In a rounded, bowllike nest, the kind a cat might make, coiled the biggest goddamn rattlesnake Longarm had ever encountered. Its wedgelike head was bigger than Longarm's fist, and its body was larger in circumference than many a man's thigh. This reptile looked as if it had ruled these lost ridges since God walked away and left the land half-finished.

For a couple of seconds the sluggish diamondback lay almost comatose in the heat. But it was not comatose. The way it writhed, coiling its huge body into itself and whipping its segmented rattles, was all the warning anyone was going to get that it was annoyed.

In fascinated horror, he watched it coil and heard the fierce, rhythmic rattle of those castanets of death. That old fellow carried enough venom in those fangs to stun a cavalry troop.

He tilted the rifle and then hesitated. A shot, among these rocks and in this immense stillness, would carry for miles. It was like calling out to Waymeyer. But there was no time to delay, either. The snake flicked its head, its eyes glittering darkly, its tongue spitting as it rocked, setting itself to spring.

Longarm slipped his hand down the barrel and inverted the rifle. With its butt, he struck the bobbing head first. The stunned reptile wavered, its huge head bloodied, its rattles singing like a thousand enraged hornets.

Longarm brought the rifle butt down again and again, until the head was smashed against the rocks. But the sound of that rifle butt on stone was as loud as gunfire in the incredible silence of the wasteland.

Longarm lifted the great reptile on his gun barrel and tossed it away among the rocks. Jesus. It was a sin to kill a specimen as amazing as that one, but the only thing more immoral than killing the rattler was being killed by it.

When Longarm palmed the rifle again and jerked his head around toward the flats and the backtrail, he saw only one rider.

Waymeyer had slowed. He still wore the kerchief across his face, and his flat-brimmed hat was still pulled down. He carried a rifle in his left hand now, and most important of all, he was suddenly alone.

Instinctively, Longarm dropped to his knee behind the small boulder. It was not much more protection than a river rock, but he crouched there, searching the two lesser ridges below them for sign of Cutlip and Gowdy. There was none.

He heard Connie's sharp intake of breath and reacted instantly, dropping to the ground and pressing against the rock.

She whispered, "Oh Custis—above you, Custis."

He heaved himself over on his back, searching the rocks above him.

Longarm sucked in an agonized breath. It was as if he gazed, wide-eyed, into the blazing furnace of the desert sun itself. His eyes seemed to fry in their sockets, and for an instant he was blind.

Something moved in that blazing yellow and orange furnace. It was like God's face. And then it wasn't God's face, but Bales Cutlip's bearded countenance, twisted in a smile of triumph.

Then he saw the rifle, socked against Cutlip's shoulder, the hand on the glittering barrel, the finger touching the trigger.

Longarm yelled like an Indian, hoping to distract Bales long enough to set himself.

Cutlip seemed as cool and confident as though Longarm were a target in a carnival shooting gallery.

Longarm's yell blasted through the rocks and rolled out across the flats.

As he yelled, he levered himself upward. Holding the rifle like a handgun, he fired twice in rapid succession.

Cutlip fired, but his bullet sailed harmlessly past the rocks where Longarm sprawled.

Longarm watched his own two slugs find their target. The first struck Cutlip in the belly and bent him forward. The second exploded in the middle of that huge and evil god's face. Bales Cutlip's features disappeared abruptly in the crimson gore. His arms relaxed on the rifle, as if obeying some terminal message. The weapon struck the rocks and clattered away among them.

Unmoving, Longarm sprawled on his back, watching the man in the rocks above him.

Cutlip poised there for an instant, and then lunged downward, as if pursuing the lost rifle. He lay twisted and buckled over the rock outcroppings. His head toppled at an odd angle over a flat stone. He did not move.

Longarm exhaled heavily. He felt as if he hadn't breathed for ten minutes. He moved his head, checking to see that Connie was all right.

She had pulled herself around on her knees, holding her gun against the rocks. She stared upward, mouth agape, watching Gowdy come down toward them, bent low, his gun ready as he steadied himself on the incline, catching at the rocks to slow himself.

Longarm jerked his rifle up, and realized it was empty. They'd only been able to find two bullets that fitted it. He dropped it instinctively and grabbed for the old gun in its holster.

As he yanked it free, he saw that he was too late. Gowdy had them in plain view from above. The stocky, bearded man had stopped up there and sunk to his knees, steadying himself, with the rifle fixed on Longarm.

Longarm sucked in a deep breath and tried to pull himself in behind a couple of shattered pebbles. There was no escape this time.

He went on yanking the old gun free and lifting it, even though he knew it was too late.

From beyond Gowdy, a rifle cracked in the sun-stunned stillness. A slug sang off the boulder beside Gowdy's head.

Longarm's heart lunged. He heard Connie's cry: "Martin—"

He heard Gowdy's startled yell, and saw the gunslick yank his head around, looking for Martin in the sagebrush below him.

Then, realizing his mistake, Gowdy turned his head around again, but he was too late.

Longarm fired. He held the old gun out in his fist and kept firing. He emptied the cylinder and kept pressing the trigger after the bullets were spent and Gowdy was dead in the rocks above them. Then he dropped the gun and called, "Connie!" He held out his hands and she tossed her loaded rifle to him.

As he moved, Noah Waymeyer fired from his saddle on the rise below them.

Longarm whirled, firing toward the Elder. Waymeyer took quick stock of his situation. His henchmen lay dead; he was alone against Longarm and Haswell, concealed in the sagebrush beyond. He quickly lost interest in the confrontation. He fired one more time, but this was almost a formality.

Longarm held his breath. He felt as if he could watch the cogs turning in the false Elder's mind. With his cronies dead, the odds had swung around, and were now against him. Retreat suddenly appeared the better part of valor. Maybe he wanted Consequence for his seventh wife, but if he didn't live to enjoy her, it would all be pointless.

He decided in that instant to return to the sanctuary of Alamut. He was in trouble, deep trouble, but he was not lost yet. He had sold those Mormon oafs a bill of goods before, and he could do it again—but all of that was predicated on one condition, that he made it alive back to the valley.

From the rocks above, Longarm watched Waymeyer suddenly thrust his rifle back in its saddle scabbard and pull the head of his animal around. Then Waymeyer raced away across the rough ground, as if the devil rode his tail.

Longarm hesitated only a few seconds. He ran down the incline and found Cutlip's horse where it had been left ground-tied.

Longarm ran to it. The horse shied, but Longarm snagged the lines as it yanked its head upward and turned to flee.

He swung into the saddle, turned the horse, and raced downward into the sage after the hard-riding Waymeyer.

Pushing the animal, Longarm lifted the rifle and fired once. The sound of the shot rolled across the glittering, sunstruck land.

He watched Waymeyer spur his horse and bend close over the animal's flying mane.

Cutlip's horse faltered, and for the first time Longarm pulled his gaze from the fleeing Elder to check the animal's condition.

When the horse missed a step, Longarm slowed it. Cutlip had already pushed the horse to the limits of its endurance. If he kept chasing Waymeyer, he might catch him in these flats, but most certainly he would kill this horse.

He saw Waymeyer glance back across his shoulder. Likely, the man's own horse was faltering.

Longarm drew rein. Hell, killing this horse was the last thing he wanted. He needed this animal for Connie. They could move more slowly now, but they could move only if Connie had a mount. After a hatful of water and an hour's rest and forage, this horse should carry Connie with no trouble the

151

remainder of the twenty-mile trek across the alkali flats. They didn't have pursuers to worry about now. All that mattered at this moment was keeping Connie off that sprained and swollen ankle, and making it to the railhead. Elder Waymeyer would return to the safety of Alamut, but that security was going to be temporary as hell; Longarm would see to that.

He swung down from the saddle. Clutching the reins, he walked slowly, letting the beaten animal plod at its own pace behind him. Waymeyer would keep. He would come back for him, with proof, with help.

When he came up the slope of the second rise, he saw Martin and Connie waiting, watching him plod toward them. Martin had rounded up Gowdy's horse and set Connie in the saddle. He had watered the horse and the burro.

"I think you scared the hell out of him," Martin said.

Longarm shrugged. "I will. Sooner or later."

Martin gave him an odd smile. "Know what I found when I went down in those flats west of here?"

"I got no idea," Longarm said.

Now Martin grinned broadly. "Hell," he said. "I found the railroad tracks."

Chapter 13

As quiet as any Sunday-morning settlement, midweek Las Vegas village sprawled prostrate in the Nevada desert heat. An artesian spring, rock-walled now, was the anemic heart of the place. The brightest spots in town were the new railroad tracks, reflecting the afternoon sun like silver. The cluster of railroad shanties, general store, saloon, and one-room depot was set down in an expanse of open desert.

No one moved in the stunning afternoon heat when Longarm walked into town, leading Connie's horse. Behind her rode Martin, with the burro in tow. Havasu Indians sprawled in the shade of building overhangs or shared the shade of the only tree in town—a gnarled Spanish oak that shaded the town well and drew its sustenance from it.

A glance as they plodded past showed the single saloon to be empty, the bartender sleeping in the shady porch overhang. A poker table was in view from the street, but it was unoccupied too.

Whatever life there was pulsed around Riley's General Store. Riley's sign advertised "Water, Victuals, Supplies, and Souvenirs." Riley himself came out on the porch crowded with bags, barrels, and resting Indians.

A stout, balding man, with the ruddy look of an Irishman about him, Riley walked to the edge of the shade and squinted at them. "Come far?" he inquired.

"Too far for comfort," Longarm replied.

"Well, that's true for anybody who wants to come to our little metropolis. Some say the sun sets 'twixt Las Vegas and civilization. We ain't exactly convenient, but we are friendly as hell. We figure folks passing on the new train line, seeing us, will stop awhile, or come back for sure." He swung his arm. "That's why I've put in a complete line of Indian relics made by the Havasu squaws theirselves—dolls, stuffed animals, bracelets."

"Got yourself a real tourist trap here," Longarm agreed. "Mind if we water our animals?"

"Help yourself, friend. Trough is free and open to a man's horse. There is no way anybody could charge a man to water his animal in this country. But the water in the artesian well is clean, for human consumption. That'll cost you a penny a pail."

Martin, having led his horse and burro to the trough, leaned over the rock wall of the spring. "This water stinks, mister," he said.

"Sure it does," Riley agreed. "But once you get it past your nose, you're all right."

Longarm glanced around. "Is there a doctor in this town? This lady has sprained her ankle."

Riley nodded. "I happen to be a kind of saddlebag sawbones. Got the latest book on human ills and the medicines to cure them. Read up well. Also, I'm good with livestock. Bring the little lady into the shade, we ought to be able to fix up that ankle as good as new. Got a good, old-fashioned liniment, excellent for man or beast. Prepared it myself."

Longarm lifted Connie down from the saddle and carried her onto the porch. Riley chased an Indian off one of the sacks of beans and nodded toward it. "Little lady ought to be comfortable there."

Riley brought a sharp butcher knife and sliced away Connie's boot. "That was a decent shoe," Longarm protested.

"I also sell ladies' boots and shoes, mister," Riley said. "You got nothing to worry about." He glanced up. "Them hacked-up relics you're wearing—about time to replace them too."

"I'll have to wait," Longarm said, "until I can wire to Denver for money."

"Happen to run the telegraph office," Riley said. "Soon's we take care of the little lady, we'll see to your wants. Can you pay for the telegram?"

"Don't have to," Longarm said. "I'll send it collect."

Riley shrugged, massaging Connie's swollen ankle. He bent her foot back and forth. She grimaced, but did not speak. "Lucky," Riley said. "It ain't broke. We'll wrap it in some cotton gauze with my liniment, and she'll be dancing the reel by tomorrow night."

Riley opened a quart mason jar, and a pungent odor spread across the stoop, strong enough to overcome the aroma of the artesian well.

"My God," Longarm said. "What is that stuff?"

Riley was liberally spreading the liniment on Connie's leg, from the knee down. He didn't get many cases like this, and he was going to get maximum entertainment value from it in effecting his cure. "Beautiful little lady," he said over his shoulder, stroking her calf and ankle.

Humming "put your little foot...put your little foot right out..." Riley rubbed in the liniment until Connie's foot and ankle glowed a bright red. "My own mixture," he told Longarm. "From an old Virginia recipe. Half an ounce of gum camphor, half an ounce saltpeter, half an ounce spirits of ammonia in half a pint of alcohol. Cures sprains, rheumatism in man or beast. And if you get in a real bind, you *can* drink it. Though honestly, I wouldn't advise that."

"My foot is burning up," Connie said.

"Yes, ma'am," Riley said. "That there's the camphor and ammonia, already at work. Then that alcohol will soothe. Let the breeze cool it a few minutes and we'll wrap it in gauze and you ought to be able to hobble pretty good."

"What breeze?" Longarm wondered.

Riley glanced up over his shoulder and grinned. "Mister, you going to live in a place like Las Vegas, you got to learn to be sensitive to the faintest breeze. Ask any of these Indians don't they feel a little cooling breeze."

"Will they understand me?"

Riley laughed. "I didn't say that." He watched Connie slump back against the rough adobe wall of his store. "You look plumb tuckered, little lady. You need a real rest."

Longarm glanced around. "Is there an inn around here, or anyone who could rent us a couple of beds?"

Riley nodded. "I happen to have ready four adobe rooms built out back. With cots. Not the best accommodations in the world, but the only ones you're going to find west of St. George."

"We'll take two of them," Longarm said.

Riley nodded. "Small windows in them rooms, but you can sleep with the door open. Get a nice cross-ventilation at night. Everybody in Las Vegas sleeps with their doors open. 'Cept for a varmint or a sidewinder wanderin' in, safe as can be." He hesitated, glancing toward Martin. "You folks *can* pay—for the water and rooms—and the emergency medical work I'm doing?"

"We'll work it out. Martin will pay his share, and I'm not going anywhere until money is wired in here to me. You'll get paid."

"Don't mean to be cheap or stingy or unneighborly," Riley said. "Last thing in this world I want. But a man has to live, you know."

"Even in Las Vegas," Longarm agreed.

Longarm wrote out his first wire to Billy Vail, and stood in the shadowy silence of the overstocked store as Riley tapped it out on the telegraph key:

COLLECT TO CHIEF U S MARSHAL VAIL FIRST DISTRICT COURT OF COLORADO DENVER STOP HAPPY TO REPORT I AM STILL ALIVE STOP DONT TRY TO COLLECT ON MY INSURANCE STOP LITTLE BILLY BATES STILL AT LARGE STOP SENT ME ON UNSCHEDULED TRIP DOWN COLORADO RIVER STOP FULL REPORT FOLLOWS COLLECT STOP SIGNED DEPUTY MARSHAL LONG

Longarm grinned at the thought of Billy Vail's reddening face when he read the phrase "FULL REPORT FOLLOWS COLLECT"; it would likely ruin his whole day.

"You really a U.S. marshal?" Riley asked.

"Sure, why?"

"You sure as hell don't look it."

"You ought to see me in my Sunday-go-to-meeting clothes," Longarm said.

156

Riley sighed, relieved. "From the looks of you, I took you for a road agent down on his luck and on the prod. I got a couple of Indians behind counters with guns on you."

"Tell them to relax."

"I don't know the Havasu word for 'relax.'"

Riley managed to get the idea across to the pair of confused Indians while Longarm composed his second message:

...SEND INFORMATION POSSIBLE CRIMINALS NAMED WAY-MEYER CUTLIP AND GOWDY STOP RECORDS MAY GO BACK 10 YEARS OR MORE STOP POSSIBLE THEY OPERATED IN BOULDER CANYON AREA STOP GOWDY AND CUTLIP DEAD BUT WAYMEYER ESCAPED STOP NOW HIDING IN ALAMUT VALLEY A MORMON SETTLEMENT STOP...

Riley sent this message as Longarm scribbled a third. The storekeeper glanced up and smiled. "You're in a real talkative mood at five cents a word."

"Been a long time since I was home," Longarm said. "Got a lot to say. You'll like the next one."

Riley took the sheet of paper on which Longarm had written his third message, and began to tap it out:

...URGENT YOU SEND FUNDS IMMEDIATELY STOP NEED CLOTHES WEAPONS FOOD TRAVEL EXPENSES LOST IN LINE OF DUTY STOP MUST BE REIMBURSED BEFORE I CAN CON-TINUE WORK OR RETURN DENVER STOP FULL REPORT FOL-LOWS...

Riley looked up, grinning. "You're going to scare the hell out of him, you keep threatening to send a full report."

"That's the idea," Longarm said. "If I get him worried that I *will* send a full report, he'll do everything else I want—and fast—to keep me from doing it."

Connie remained stretched out on a croker sack of navy beans on the stoop. Martin sat in a backless straight chair beside her when Longarm came out of the store. The Havasus stared at them, unblinking, curious, and impressed. They had never seen anyone quite like them before.

Martin said, "Did you ask him how much he'd give us for two horses, two saddles, and a burro?"

"My God." Longarm shook his head. "I didn't even think about it."

"We can't eat 'em, and I sure don't want to take them with us to Salt Lake City. And I don't think you'd want to ride one of them back into Alamut Valley."

"That's right. As soon as I get authorization from Denver, I can rent horse and gear."

"Are you really going back to Alamut?" Connie said.

"I really am," Longarm said.

Riley had followed him out of the store. He walked down the step to the blistered street and inspected the horses and burro. He named his price, just this side of highway robbery. When Martin protested, Riley said, "Even a few dollars is better than eatin' 'em."

Longarm said, "You keep cheating people like this, Riley, you never will get any tourists in Las Vegas."

Riley shrugged smiling equably. "Tourists *live* to be cheated," he said.

"I hope so," Longarm told him. "For your sake."

Martin said, "We'll throw in three rifles and those pack pouches. How much? And remember, you take those horses at what you suggest, they'll hang you for horse-stealing."

Riley smiled serenely. "I figure anything you folks make on this deal is clear profit. I don't ask no questions. You don't ask no questions. Tell you what I'll do. I'll give you a hundred and a quarter for the whole shebang, and I'll throw in my medical work, the liniment, and a new pair of high-button boots for the little lady. That's my best offer."

Martin glanced at Longarm, who nodded. "We'll take it," Martin said. "We need two tickets for Salt Lake City on the next eastbound."

Riley nodded. "I can handle that for you."

"When does the next train pass through?" Martin asked.

"You're in luck, young fellow. Train is due in here at half past seven in the morning. Got sleepers and a dining coach. Latest equipment."

"You don't own the railroad too, do you?" Longarm inquired.

"Not yet." Riley laughed and shook his head. "Not yet."

They didn't get much in cash from Riley. Connie wanted a new cotton print dress that Riley had hanging over the till to entice his female clientele. Longarm bought Levi's, a flannel shirt, a flat-crowned stetson, and high-country riding boots. After his low-heeled cavalry stovepipes, the riding boots were pure misery, but following a soak in the bath house behind Riley's—one dollar, including soap, towel, shaving gear, and talcum powder—he felt almost human.

Connie was exhausted, and Martin suggested she might want to go out to their room and rest, after a bath.

"Be hot out there during the afternoon," Riley said, "but you do look tired, little lady."

Martin swung Connie up in his arms and carried her out to the bath house. As they went, Longarm could feel Connie's intense gaze upon him, but he did not look toward her.

When Martin and Connie were gone, Riley grinned and winked. "Little lady kind of hot around the edges for you, huh, Long?"

"You son of a bitch," Longarm said. "I'm her father."

Longarm's eight-by-ten crib of adobe and pine out behind Riley's store was like an oven. He managed to breathe long enough to dress in there, but he gasped as he stepped outside into the westering sun.

The sounds of gasping, sweet groaning, and the dry squealing of cot springs erupted from the crib shared by Connie and Martin. They seemed not to care about the desert heat; they even generated their own.

Longarm felt himself begin to sweat in warmth that had nothing to do with the blaze of desert sun, the blast of furnacelike wind. He thought about Connie's bare, beautiful, and supple body, whether he wanted to or not. The way he had possessed her, totally and passionately, was too new in his mind to be denied. Connie materialized, naked and voluptuous and alluring, behind his eyes. In his mind he nursed her breasts, caressed that smooth and pliant form, felt her eager hands and lips reaching for him . . .

Exhaling, he strode away from the adobe cribs, going around the side of the store. He doubted there was a pliable female within the environs of Las Vegas. He wondered if there ever would be . . .

His belly felt empty, his nerves were drawn taut like singing barbed wire, and his loins ached. The memory of Connie's passion trailed him, haunted him, making him move faster.

He paused beside the well, under the wan shade of the gnarled oak, and glanced around; this was the only tree, except for stubby, miniature pinyons and junipers lost among the sage, as far as he could see.

He shook his head. This was a hot, dead land, ugly and without promise, rimmed by scorching hills that reared, almost lost in the distance. The heat tortured his eyes, and his vision tormented his brain. The whole limitless expanse of desert shimmered, as unreal as any mirage. The railroad tracks, twisting east past the water tower and glittering west, seemed suspended in blue heat waves, unmoored, insubstantial, and floating. The telegraph poles and wires stretched into nothingness, as if trying to tie it all together.

Slumped in the shade of the oak, he tried to reach out in his mind to the reality east and west and north of here, but even the memory of it eluded him in this unreal place, drifting far beyond those jagged hills marking remote horizons. He let his gaze search the scant sagebrush, and then move on. A direct line west showed him that nineteen-thousand-foot peak they'd used to guide them to this place. The far mountain swam in gray mist, untouchable and unreachable in this desert heat.

Beyond the flats of sagebrush lay open gravel ridges like the wrinkles of a metal washboard, and as bare. He stared across the desert toward that lone mountain peak, drifting in mists, red and gray and gleaming now as the sun lowered.

He dropped a penny into the coffee can beside the public long-handled dipper, and filling the pail, he drank of the cold water. He watched faint clouds brave the bare expanses of bleached skies.

Riley came out on the porch with a yellow paper in his hand. He said, "Mr. Long, here's an answer to your telegrams."

Longarm nodded. He crossed the sunlit yard to the porch, his feet aching in the high-heeled riding boots. He stepped up into the shade and took the telegrams.

Riley shook his head. "Your daughter—and her husband—are having one hell of a time out back, ain't they?"

Longarm stared down at him. "They're on their honeymoon, Riley. Weren't you ever young?"

"I'm still young," Riley said. "It's just that I got nobody but my fist."

The telegram was written in Vail's usual spare style:

TO DEPUTY U S MARSHAL LONG LAS VEGAS STOP DO NOT
REPEAT DO NOT WIRE FULL REPORT STOP AUTHORIZING
PAYMENT 50 DOLLARS STOP YOU MUST BE MORE CAREFUL
WITH YOUR BELONGINGS STOP RECORDS FOUND ON WAY-
MEYER CUTLIP AND GOWDY STOP FEDERAL OFFENSES STOP
MORE LATER STOP DO NOT WIRE AGAIN UNLESS LIFE OR
DEATH STOP VAIL U S MARSHAL DENVER

Riley grinned. "Sounds like a real nice fellow to work for,"
he said.

"Pure government issue," Longarm said.

Riley handed him a gold eagle and two double eagles.
"Come on in," he said. "Fix you right up."

"At your prices?" Longarm said. "Are you crazy?"

Longarm slept only fitfully in the hot desert night. He awoke
often, restless and sweating, on the flat cot. He breathed deeply,
searching for a full breath of air, but the still night air burned
his nostrils and dried his throat.

But if he slept badly, Connie and Martin slept not at all.
Every time he woke in the darkness, he heard Martin and
Connie gasping and panting in the next crib. He hoped Haswell
would have strength enough to board the eastbound in the
morning.

He finally plunged into deep sleep in the false dawn. He
was wakened by Riley's shaking his shoulder at six o'clock.
"Best get up," Riley said, "if you want to see your daughter
off on the eastbound. Got a message, the eastbound is on time
this morning. Right on the dot. It will stop only long enough
to take on passengers and jerk water."

Yawning, Longarm got up, dressed in his new duds, and
forced his aching feet into the riding boots.

Martin and Connie awaited him in the early-morning sunlight. The heat was already intense.

"We might as well get on over to the depot," Martin said.

Connie smiled at Longarm. "I want to thank you, Custis,
for getting us this far. I know Martin and I will be happy in
Salt Lake City."

"I hope so," Martin said. "I can tell you I'm plenty scared,
leaving home like this for the first time in my life."

They crossed the wide, hard-packed main street and sat on

crates at the depot. Just as they heard the train whistle in the distance, Connie said, "Martin, we forgot your gun and holster."

"We won't need it in Salt Lake City."

"I want you to have it," she said. "I'll feel safer."

Reluctantly, Martin glanced along the tracks toward the west. The train was still not in sight, but they heard its whistle again in the still morning. He ran around the depot and across the street.

Connie watched him go. "We'll have a nice wedding in Salt Lake, Custis. And it will all be thanks to you—for everything."

"I just want you to be happy," he said, watching the rails where the train would appear.

She sighed heavily and whispered, "I'll always love you, Custis."

He turned and gazed at her. "You concentrate on Martin. On making him happy. Even if there was a chance for us, I'm not the marrying kind. You are. Martin is. And besides, I'm likely older than Noah Waymeyer. You go with Martin and be happy."

"I'll give Martin all I can." Inwardly, Longarm grinned, assured that she would. Her voice raked at him like kitten claws. "But you're in my heart, Custis, I can't help that."

He smiled. "You're in my heart too, Connie, but Martin deserves the best."

"He'll get more than he deserves," she said with a flat smile. "Maybe even more than he'll want. But maybe sometimes when he is having me, I'll be lying there, remembering you. He'll think I'm wild, and won't know why. That's all right, isn't it? If Martin never suspects?"

Longarm sighed. "If Martin never suspects," he said in a firm tone.

He kissed her goodbye, and they were standing like friends saying casual farewells when Martin returned along the freight platform.

When the train was gone, Longarm walked back across the street. It was not even eight o'clock and it was already hotter than the hinges of hell.

Riley awaited him on the porch of the general store, and handed him another telegram:

162

...STAY IN LAS VEGAS AND AWAIT ARRIVAL OF DEPUTY MARSHAL TOM CRAIG FROM SALT LAKE CITY STOP CRAIG HAS EXPERIENCE DEALING WITH MORMONS AND WILL HAVE FULL DETAILS ON WAYMEYER STOP CLOSE THIS CASE AND RESUME PURSUIT OF LITTLE BILLY BATES...

Longarm looked around at the desolate settlement, and swore. "Well," he said, "I'm stuck here for a while. My God. Even a drink of water costs money here."

Riley laughed. "Hell, you'll enjoy your visit here, as long as you stay in the shade. Ask any of these Indians."

Chapter 14

Deputy U.S. Marshal Tom Craig awed the usually unflappable Longarm because the lawman from Salt Lake City presented, from his hat to his boots, the perfect government official. His gray felt hat was not new, but it was brushed and cared for, and it was a genuine Stetson. He obviously wore it in every kind of inclement weather, but just as obviously he took care of it, as he did the other tools of his trade and apparel. His flannel shirt was pressed, and his string tie was knotted with a small silver ring. His trousers were saddle-slicked, but well cut and of good quality. His boots were size twelve at least. His legs were heavy, maybe a little short for this thick, long trunk, and his chest bulged the fabric of his shirt, and his huge shoulders strained his tweed jacket. He wore his gun in a holster just below his natural belt line, and even this weapon looked used, but respected and cared for.

Craig's steak-fed face, sun-varnished and coldly serene, also must have given many a lawbreaker pause.

The crowded meeting house at Alamut was loud and crackling with rage when Craig strode in, followed by Longarm. Some of the men shouted insults at Longarm and the stranger, but Craig merely walked to the middle of the raised platform

165

where the Elders' table was placed. He stood there, unmoving and unsmiling, until the settlers grew quiet, uneasy, and a little troubled at his granitelike countenance.

Longarm gazed at those faces. The Alamut meeting house was as jammed with the faithful as it had been the day Longarm was tried and convicted in this room. Every pine bench was filled. As it had been that first time, the room was filled with angered, prejudiced farmers who began with fear and distrust of outsiders and built their venom from there.

One didn't have to be a seer to read the silent, cold support for Elder Noah Waymeyer in those rigid faces.

The twelve chairs at the Elders' table were empty. Deputy Marshal Tom Craig stood alone at the center of the table, and Longarm sat in a chair pushed against the wall.

When Tom Craig didn't speak at once, some older men in the audience took the offensive.

"Why have you come back here, Gentile?" they shouted at Longarm.

Tom Craig's voice was sharp, authoritative, and, like his gun, a weapon to instill respect. "I am a deputy U.S. marshal. My name is Tom Craig. I am here for two reasons: one is official and the other is a part of my religion—and yours. I want to help you people if I can."

"If you wanted to help us, why did you bring this Antichrist back to our valley with you?"

Tom Craig's face almost pulled into a faint smile but not quite. "I didn't bring Long; Long brought *me*. If you people had any sense of justice and gratitude, you'd be thanking him—"

"For what? For stealing one of our women?"

"The woman who left this place, left willingly," Craig said.

"This Antichrist spread the devil's evil doctrine into the mind and heart of our son Martin Haswell."

"Martin Haswell will marry the woman Consequence Knight, whom he took from this place. To come and go, that is a freedom promised to all of us. Martin and Consequence decided to go. As many of you know in your hearts, they had good and sufficient reason for wanting to leave this valley. They are about to be married and are living now in Salt Lake City."

There was a faint buzz of chatter among the women, quickly silenced.

An Elder shouted, "Are you going to tell us that this devil, Long, didn't kill two of Elder Noah Waymeyer's trusted lieutenants?"

Tom Craig stared the questioner down. The man cleared his throat and looked around, uncomfortable.

Craig's voice raked at him. "I am going to tell you this about Custis Long. He is exactly what he has told you people all along he was: a deputy U.S. marshal. He didn't have to come back here, but he wanted to, because he wanted to help you people, if he could—despite what you have done to him."

A man shouted, "Long has opposed Elder Waymeyer. He shot at him. He killed his trusted workers. We owe Elder Waymeyer our loyalty."

"All right." Craig's voice lashed at them like a whip, cracked just above their heads. "Let's consider this Elder Waymeyer, to whom you swear you owe your loyalty. For what do you owe him loyalty? For deceiving you? For robbing you? He robbed you gullible people for ten years, just as, before that, he robbed the U.S. government—with guns.

"It is precisely because of his career as road agent, bandit, and killer that Noah Waymeyer came to you here in Alamut Valley in the first place, along with two surviving members of his gang."

"Gang?" somebody yelled. "He came to us from the Tabernacle at—"

"Noah Waymeyer was never anywhere near Salt Lake City. He is not a Mormon, nor related to a Mormon, nor descended from a Mormon. Waymeyer was part of what was called the Boulder Canyon gang—ten years ago. They terrorized the three states around here, and hid out in this wild Boulder Canyon country. Their last criminal assault as a gang was an attack on a government pay train. They got money, they got what they were after, but in the fighting they were almost totally wiped out. All the others of the Boulder Canyon gang were found dead or were accounted for—except Waymeyer, Cutlip, and Gowdy. These three men disappeared in the desert. They were never found. They were presumed dead by the U.S. government, and their case was marked closed—until a few weeks ago."

The people stared up at Tom Craig in stunned silence. They didn't want to believe him, but there was no doubting the sincerity and authority of that cold, unyielding voice. He paused, scanning the faces before him, then went on:

"How could you people have permitted Waymeyer to force you to turn over one-third of your crops to him as tithe? How? Are all of you that stupid? All of you? Even the oldest among you? Don't any of you know that tithing is ten percent? Ten percent!"

"Elder Waymeyer threatened to excommunicate those of us who protested," someone said. "He said the Church at Salt Lake was in trouble and needed all it could get from all of us."

Tom Craig shook his head. "Have none of you been out of this valley? Have none of you returned, even in a pilgrimage, to Salt Lake City? Have none of you witnessed the wonders the Church has accomplished there? Well, of course, the answer is obvious.

"In the first place, he could *demand* nothing of you, even as your elected spiritual leader. Tithing is not compulsory—in Salt Lake Valley or anywhere else. Tithing is totally a voluntary expression of one's devout loyalty to his Church.

"And that brings us to the woman Consequence Knight, who you say was spirited from this valley by Custis Long. As tithing is totally voluntary in our church, so is marriage. There is nothing in *The Book of Mormon* about any woman being forced against her will to marry anyone. And yet that is what you allowed Noah Waymeyer to do here. He wanted to force Consequence to wed him. Instead she ran away with the man she loved.

"Are these crimes enough to convince you that you owe no loyalty to Noah Waymeyer? There is certainly more. In our Church, Mormon Elders are expected to pay their own way. They are not permitted to tax their congregations as Noah taxed you people. They are not allowed to live off the sweat and labors of others—as Waymeyer lived here."

He exhaled heavily and said, "I can understand why you settlers out here—far from your Church and your people—behaved as you did, why you followed a false prophet. You lived here isolated, alone, afraid of outsiders. You wanted to believe the Church cared enough to send you a strong leader. You wanted to believe your leader came out from the temple in Salt Lake City to defend and protect you. Well, he didn't.

"I've said none of this to shame or hurt you people. But I was obliged to explain to you that Mr. Long and I are going out to Elder Waymeyer's home to arrest him."

A faint stir rippled across the crowd, the residue of ten years of blind loyalty.

Tom Craig said, "I must advise you people, you will be punished severely—by the U.S. government—if you interfere with Mr. Long and me in the execution of our duties. Noah Waymeyer will be arrested on a federal warrant. He will return with me to Salt Lake City to face federal criminal charges. I am sorry, but that is why we are here."

There was a taut, protracted silence, and then Elder Abel McFee stood up, tall and Lincolnesque, in the crowd. He spoke in a soft, sad voice: "I'll go along with you."

Elder Regis Hill stood up too. "And I," Hill said. He was joined by his sons, and then by several others.

Tom Craig thanked them. "And the rest of you people return to your homes. Soon Alamut Valley will be quiet again, and you can return to your productive lives—under new and honest leaders."

The posse rode into the yard of the large adobe house where Noah Waymeyer had lived these past years with his growing number of wives.

The women came out on the veranda. Longarm stared at them. One could see by their ages that Waymeyer had married his first wife because she was some Elder's unmarried daughter—a politic thing to do while he was establishing his base in the valley. Each of his other wives looked younger and prettier, and Connie would have been the loveliest of all. Waymeyer had plucked the finest cherries each season. But at the moment the women wept, inconsolable, shaking their heads when Craig asked for Waymeyer.

"He's gone," the oldest of the six wives said. The other women wept afresh, whether at the loss of their husband, or of their security, one could not say.

"Did he say where he was going?" Craig asked.

The woman shook her head. "He only cursed us when we tried to question him. He said he would never come back. We will never see him again."

"How long ago did he leave?" Craig said.

The oldest wife sniffled. "He began to pack his bag when word was brought to him that the Gentile had returned."

"The mountain pass," Elder McFee said. "If he had very much to carry, it is the only way out. Perhaps the guards—"

169

"They would not dare try to stop the Elder," Hill said.

"Maybe not," Craig said. "But it is a chance we must take." He jerked his head toward McFee. "Why don't you lead the way, Elder? And you needn't spare the horses."

The posse wheeled about in the yard and raced away from the women, weeping and abandoned on the rich veranda of the great old house.

Longarm was the last to turn his horse, the last to gallop out of the yard. Some instinct, born of his long experience in tracking down malefactors, warned him that Waymeyer was too smart to attempt to leave via the guarded pass to the south.

He slowed his horse, letting the posse race ahead of him. He didn't believe Waymeyer had carried much from the house. The posse had assumed he had taken large quantities of goods when they heard the words "he began to pack." But had he?

Longarm chewed at that. If Waymeyer was smart— and whatever else Longarm thought of him, he conceded that the ex-Elder was a smart criminal—he must have known his defrauding of the settlers couldn't last forever. He had killed to ensure his safety, but all the time he must have known there would come a day when the gravy train would spring a leak.

What would a felon do in a situation like that? *What would I do?* Longarm mused. *I know what I would do. I would stash away my fortune someplace where I could get to it, where it would be hidden and secure, and ready when I had to run for my life.*

Without even really knowing why he did it, Longarm found himself turning his horse and heading it due north as the posse thundered away at top speed in the other direction.

He could not dismiss the idea of that goat path over which he and Martin and Connie had escaped the valley. Martin had said it was known to most of the settlers, but it would still offer an escape route when any pursuers thought one would ride south through the pass.

He angled across the fields, quiet in the blazing sun, as the workers all gathered in the village to discuss their tragedy.

As he climbed toward that ridge where Martin had led them over the high cliffs, a strange silence enveloped him along with the burning sun, the cutting wind. No animal moved in the rocks, no bird shrilled from the thickets. Alert, Longarm straightened in his saddle, searching the faces of the cliffs for any puffs of dust that might be raised by his quarry as he sought to escape. He saw nothing.

He lowered his head, looking for the break in the rocks that was the single guidepost to the path. He found the ragged slash in the base of the cliff.

His heart lunged. He might have missed the path, but for a whisper of sound above him. The noise was almost nothing, a pebble loosened to clatter in the rocks.

He jerked his head up, and saw where the goat trail writhed upward toward the rocky crest.

He halted his horse and swung down from the saddle, wishing he was wearing his low-heeled cavalry stovepipes. But this wisp of a thought merely fled through his conscious mind while he searched the rocks above him.

He moved around the larger boulders and started up the narrow path, leading his horse. He knew from Martin's experience that hazing an animal over this path was tedious and risky, but if Waymeyer was already beyond this ridge, he would need the horse. He sure as hell couldn't walk far in these man-killing boots.

He had gone less than a hundred feet, struggling on the sheer, flat rocks, when a rifle blasted from the ledge above him.

Longarm heard the dull *splat* of the bullet, a direct hit between the eyes of his horse. The animal trembled, shuddered, retreated a step, and then crumpled, dead.

Cursing, Longarm pressed in under the slight overhang of a boulder. That shot had been carefully planned. Kill the horse first, and take care of the man later. He cursed again as he realized that the horse had fallen on its right side, pinning Longarm's rifle, in its saddle scabbard, under its heavy body. Even if Longarm could wrestle the rifle loose, he didn't dare expose himself long enough to accomplish the task. He would have to make do with the second-hand Colt .44 he had purchased from Riley in Las Vegas. At least it had a full-length barrel, as opposed to his own Colt Model T, lost in the flooded streets of Carp.

Fat lot of good it'll do you, old son, he told himself ruefully, *against a man with a rifle, and elevation on you to boot.*

Crouched on the slate bed and pressed in under the jutting stone, Longarm held his gun ready, searching the winding path above him.

171

He caught the faint glint of sunlight off a gun barrel in the path fifty or sixty feet above him.

Then he saw the horse, struggling, its head up and tail flying as it slipped and stumbled in the sheer climb. Bent low in front of the animal, using it as a shield against anyone behind and below him, Waymeyer scurried upward.

Longarm was already clambering between the rocks, running along the trail, staying as low as he could and still move his legs. A bullet whistled past his head and he dove forward on his face.

He stayed there a moment until he saw that Waymeyer was climbing again, yanking the reins of the horse as he went.

Lying there, taking aim, Longarm fired. He heard the horse screech in pain and rear tall. It staggered backward and fell.

Waymeyer looked around wildly, like a cornered rat. Longarm could not understand how the man had believed he would not try to even the odds between them. One dead horse, two dead horses. Two men afoot in the cliffs.

Waymeyer fired again. Longarm dug in behind some small rocks, awaiting another shot. But it did not come.

Cautiously and slowly he lifted his head.

His mouth gaped open. The leftover panic from that moment when he had lost his henchmen in the desert confrontation must have incapacitated the outlaw's thinking processes.

Waymeyer had left the goat path and was clambering upward through the rock outcroppings. Longarm watched in disbelief.

He aimed his sixgun, steadying it in both hands, and fired upward. Waymeyer didn't even look back.

Longarm cursed. Bullets fired upward like that were damned near harmless; they seldom penetrated a target with force enough to do any damage.

He went running up the trail. This changed everything. Waymeyer was climbing, secure in the knowledge that unless Longarm got a clean shot at him, he was not even going to be winged. Then why was he climbing upward toward the crest of the ridges, instead of fleeing along the path?

Longarm ran faster. He had that answer too. Whatever it was that had brought Waymeyer up here was stashed away on the crest of these ridges somewhere, and he was on his way to collect it. The outlaw felt certain that while he could shoot downward fatally with his rifle, Longarm was almost helpless with his sixgun.

Pressed against a boulder, Longarm watched the lone man clamber upward in the rocks. Once, Waymeyer slipped and rolled downward in a small landslide. He landed against a boulder and hung there a moment, getting his breath back. He had dropped his rifle when he fell. He leaped up and climbed again, not even bothering to look for the weapon.

As if mesmerized, Longarm came from behind the boulder. He left the path, climbing upward, his gun holstered.

Gunfire rattled from a ledge above him. His face contorted, Waymeyer stood up there, firing a full magazine. Bullets splatted into rocks or sang against boulders. Longarm hit the ground and wriggled upward.

After a moment, Longarm lifted his head and saw the man climbing upward again against the sheer face of the cliff.

Up there, it was hand-over-hand climbing. A climber found a footing, caught rocks or small growth above, and then inched upward.

Longarm hesitated. There was no way he could shoot Waymeyer from here. At best, his bullets would glance off rocks, possibly even off Waymeyer at this elevation. On the other hand, Waymeyer could reach the crest first and pick Longarm off as he struggled toward the rimrock.

If you had a lick of sense, you'd back up, Longarm told himself. The odds were stacked against him. They were all with Waymeyer. Caution and common sense dictated a retreat to the path. Let Waymeyer collect whatever he sought up here, and then get him as he tried to come back to the path and move either way on it.

Longarm stared upward, squinting against the sun. Waymeyer moved sure-footedly against the facing of the cliff, not far now from the summit.

Longarm swore; he didn't want to lose the son of a bitch. There was the matter of that sentence to hard labor, and the attempts on his life. Longarm *wanted* him.

He reached upward. Carelessly, he had watched Waymeyer, and turned his thoughts inward, when this sheer climb demanded every ounce of concentration and the full attention of all his senses.

He felt a rock break free under his right boot and spin downward in space. Longarm felt himself slipping.

Just beyond his left hand grew a stunted juniper. Like most of the vegetation in this strange, hot land, the tree was a min-

173

iature. Its trunk was sturdy at the base, but it hung out over the rocks helplessly. It looked old, and as he clutched at it, Longarm prayed the juniper had sunk its roots deep into the crevices of these rocks—hell, down to China would be great.

The tiny, rough-barked tree bent and shuddered, but it held. Breathing through his mouth, he cautiously punched his toe along the outcroppings, seeking a foothold.

The world spun dizzily below him. He closed his eyes, not wanting to see the rocks jutting upward, a lethal net to catch him when he fell.

The juniper trembled again, loosened by Longarm's weight and the pull of gravity. Longarm yelled involuntarily.

From above him he heard triumphant laughter.

The juniper held, still quivering. Longarm looked around for a purchase, but found nothing. Clinging to the trembling little brush, Longarm stared upward.

Waymeyer was only a few feet from the crest, but Longarm offered too tempting a target, hanging on to the stunted tree by one hand.

Still laughing, Waymeyer took one-handed aim with his rifle. "See you in hell, Long," he yelled.

He shifted up there, turning enough to take aim and hang on to the rocks with one hand.

I'm damned if I'll let him kill me without trying, Longarm thought in fierce savagery. *This damned bush isn't going to hold anyway. What have I got to lose?*

Swinging there, hanging like an ape by his left-handed grip on the juniper, Longarm aimed his own gun as Waymeyer fired twice. Then, turning, Waymeyer lost his balance and screamed. He slipped, hanging out over the rocks, a clean target as Longarm held on and emptied his gun upward.

One moment he was hanging in the rocks up there. The next he was plunging out, spinning toward the rocks below.

Longarm swallowed back the bile that gorged up through his throat. He released his gun, letting it clatter to the rocks far down the side of the cliff. He pulled himself in close to the sheer rockface, found a footing, and pressed there, shivering.

Chapter 15

Stepping off the westbound Union Pacific limited onto the half-lit station platform at Carp, Nevada, Longarm felt an eerie sense of *déjà vu*.

This *had* happened to him before—damned near fatally. And here he was, back in town. The settlement lay dark except for Humble Earl's—the place that never closed, the rotten heart of this little hellhole.

One thing Longarm found thankfully different: there was no rain tonight, no threat of rain, in the furnace-dry desert midnight.

And there was another difference, less vital, but important to Longarm because his attire, like his guns, had always been part of his arsenal. When he'd arrived in the rain at Carp that first time, he'd been decked out in clothing that had been chosen from long experience to help him move fluidly, to keep him comfortable and make him look good—from hat and frock coat to comfortable, low-heeled cavalry boots. He'd been a man who, dressed as he was and at well over six feet tall, stood out in any crowd. Tonight, no one on the train gave him more than a cursory glance. In denim shirt and Levi's, a cheap hat, high-country boots that hurt all the way up behind his eyes, and carrying a battered satchel, Longarm looked much like any other range tramp.

He stood on the edge of the platform and watched the westbound cough and gather steam and roll away along the tracks, its wan headlamp boring a transient tunnel in the unyielding blackness.

He didn't bother glancing around at the town. He knew there was no chance of seeing either its buildings or any varmints—human or otherwise—lurking in its deep shadows.

When he turned his head, he saw the stationmaster moving around inside the lighted waiting room. This time, Longarm didn't even bother to try to enter. He knew from sad experience that that door would be locked at this hour.

He told himself grimly that he knew all he needed to know about Carp by this time—more, really, than he cared to know.

He also anticipated the station manager's next move and calmly awaited it, standing at the rim of light from the platform lantern.

The light inside the waiting room was extinguished.

Longarm moved. He drew a deep breath, held it, and padded across the platform as the stationmaster emerged through the freight doors, large brass key ready in his hand.

Before the man could touch the sliding door to pull it closed, Longarm thrust the gun in his back. The man gasped and managed to bite back a yell. "You yell, old son, and you're one dead stationmaster. Now let's just stand quiet." He took the brass key from the trembling hand.

The man shook his head. "You're all wrong, mister. I got no money here. No valuables at all."

"Your life valuable?"

"It's all I got."

"Then you might want to do what I tell you to do, and keep your mouth shut."

"Sounds just like what I want to do. But like I say there's nothing here worth—"

"I'm not looking for money. I'm looking for you."

"Me? What in the goldarn name of goodness would anybody want with an old critter like me?"

"Everybody's tastes are different, I reckon."

Slowly, his arms raised, the station manager turned. His eyes widened. The blood drained down from his head, leaving his leathery face ashen. He stared at Longarm, recognized him, refused to believe his own eyes, and then registered stunned shock, which left his mouth agape, his whole body slumping inside his overalls.

"What's wrong, old son?" Longarm inquired.

The old man had to swallow twice before he could speak at all. "You're—dead. They killed you."

"They sure as hell *tried,* didn't they?" Longarm unhooked the lantern from its peg and motioned with his gun. "Back inside, brother. You and I are going to be here awhile."

The man stepped through the sliding doors into the barely furnished freight room. "What you want with me? I ain't done nothing to you."

"I don't remember it that way. You were pretty snotty. Letting me stand out in a rainstorm."

"Yeah. But goldarn it, I done you a favor too. Tried to. I warned you to git on out of town afore they kilt you. You wouldn't listen. 'Cause you're bull-headed, that ain't my fault."

"You knew I was looking for Little Billy Bates last time. What you think I want now?"

"God knows, mister."

"Little Master Bates is still hiding out here in Carp, ain't he?"

"Ain't no place on this earth he'd be safer."

"That was true until tonight, Pop."

"My God, won't you never learn? Don't you know Billy's friends ain't going to let you live long enough to take Billy?"

"I got a pretty good idea last time, old fellow. This time it's going to be different. I'm getting on that eastbound in the morning, and Billy Bates will be with me. Now if you were a betting man, I think you'd like to wager on that."

The old man slumped down on a dirty bale of cotton. "Hell, I'd of bet you *was* dead." He shook his head, watching Longarm. "You want Billy. What you want with me?"

"I'm pleased to tell you, you old weasel. I'm going to call on Billy—over at Humble Earl's—but it's going to be on my schedule. Meantime, I'm just as happy if he and his fat harpy and misguided friends don't even know I'm back in town. So, till just before daybreak, you and I are going to sit in here. That way I won't have to worry about Billy Bates accidentally finding out that I'm not only alive, but that I've come back to Carp looking for him."

"Why, hell! You don't have to worry about me tellin'—"

"That's right, I don't." Longarm stuffed cotton in the stationmaster's mouth until the man's eyes widened. Then he tied his handkerchief around the man's mouth, gagging him. He tied the manager's arms between his legs and brought the short length of rope up over the fellow's shoulders and tied it off at the nape of his neck. "Try and make yourself comfortable," Longarm said.

He turned down the lantern wick, and blew out the small blue flame. The room and the world were plunged into darkness.

Longarm walked to the barred window that overlooked Main Street. He stood unmoving, staring at the lights of Humble Earl's saloon.

When the first shafts of crimson and purple daylight shattered the dark rim of the Mormon Range in the distance, Longarm returned to the window and stared far down the street toward the town livery stable.

He remained unmoving until a lone figure emerged from the stable and shuffled toward Humble Earl's. He recognized Crazy Charlie Wilkes. He remembered him well.

He glanced toward the station manager. The exhausted man slept, crouched on the filthy bale of hay.

Longarm drew his gun and picked up the set of iron shackles he'd had packed in his satchel, and walked past him. He went out the freight door, and closed and locked it with the brass key. Then he dropped the key into his pocket and walked around the station and crossed Main Street.

When Crazy Charlie Wilkes turned the corner, heading for the rear door of Humble Earl's, Longarm stepped from a shadowed alcove. He punched his sixgun low in Charlie's kidney and said, "You yell, Charlie, and you're dead."

Charlie stared at Longarm and recognized him. A damp patch appeared on his pants, extending slowly from his crotch down to his knees.

"Just about six o'clock, wouldn't you say, Charlie?"

Wilkes nodded, unable to speak.

"Same time you walk in that back door every morning of the world, huh?"

"Yessir. I reckon."

"Hell, Charlie, you're too modest. They set their clocks by

you arriving through that back door at Humble Earl's every morning."

"I reckon."

"Well, we're not going to disappoint them, Charlie. No, sir, not this morning. You're going to walk in there, just like you always do. Only difference is, I'm right behind you, with this pistol in your back. Anybody makes a move to get me, Charlie, I get you first."

"Oh, my God. You can't do that. That ain't human."

"Stomping me unconscious and throwing me in Meadow Valley Wash seems real human to you, huh, Charlie?"

"I didn't do that."

"But that's the way it is, Charlie. You run with the wolves, you get shot for a wolf."

A kind of stunned, early-morning pall hung over the brightly lit saloon when Crazy Charlie pushed open the back door and stepped inside. Only a few people glanced toward him, so accustomed were they to his arrival precisely at six every morning. By the time they realized Crazy Charlie Wilkes wasn't alone, it was too late.

Longarm nudged Charlie ahead of him, holding the gun where everyone could see it. Silence spread like molasses across the room.

Longarm jerked his head toward the proprietor. "All right, Humble Earl. You first. Out from behind that bar. You touch a hideout, or anything else back there, you're a dead son of a bitch."

"Hold it, Long," Humble Earl said. "I don't know how in hell you came back from the dead, but that's good enough for me."

He came around the bar and sat down at a table in plain view of Longarm. He wiped his hands on his streaked and stained apron.

Most of the men in the room were too stunned to speak or react for the moment. In the silence, Fishtail Fanny Fawkes's voice rang out: "Well, goddamm it, Billy Bates, look who's here. You should of killed him. I told you you should of killed him."

"Shut up, Fanny," Bates said in his wheedling tenor. "You just shut up."

Billy Bates turned in his chair. He laid his cards down precisely, taking his time. He grinned at Longarm. "You don't learn real fast, do you, old feller?"

"You're the slow learner, Billy. Even you ought to know your luck had to run out sometime in this town."

Billy went on grinning. "Oh, you think my luck has run out here in Carp, do you?"

"Looks like it, Billy. You got no friends to back you, because I'll bet you, Billy, there ain't a man in this room wants to take a chance on catching a bullet for you." Longarm tilted his head. "Any takers? Anybody want to step in? Make your move."

They stared at him, but nobody moved. They kept their hands on the tables, in plain sight.

Slowly, keeping Crazy Charlie at an angle in front of him, Longarm moved between the tables to where Billy sat.

"It's a long way from here to that train, Long," Billy said. "Why don't you just call it off and set down, and we'll have a few hands of five-card till train time. Then we'll all come over and see you off." He laughed but it was the only laughter in the room. Everybody else sat unmoving, watching them.

Longarm grinned back at Billy, but spoke to Fishtail Fanny: "I better warn you, Miss Fishtail. A man hates to shoot a lady, but I got no such qualms about you. I remember clear your parasol tip in my eye."

"Why, that was an accident," Billy Bates said. "You know Miss Fanny wouldn't do anything like—"

"I know Miss Fanny would kill a lot faster even than you, Little Billy. She's got more guts than you. She's also got more sense. I hope she's got sense enough to know I'll shoot her if she so much as moves her fat ass."

Fishtail Fanny winced. Her face paled faintly. She did not move.

"All right, Charlie," Longarm said. "The next few moves are up to you."

"My God, Mr. Long, what you want of me?"

"I want you on your knees, Charlie. That's right, there in front of Little Billy. Now you take these leg irons." He handed Charlie the leg irons. "And you fit 'em on Little Billy's ankles. Real nice and snug. Don't mind about bitin' into his skin. He had his chance to go with me nice and friendly, but he wouldn't have it. This time we'll do it my way, eh, Charlie?"

Little Billy watched Charlie secure the leg irons at his ankles. He stared up at Longarm, his evil face twisted. "We still ain't on that train."

Longarm ignored the shriveled little road agent. He gave Charlie a pair of handcuffs. Then he glanced at Bates. "Now, Billy boy, if you'll just put both your arms around your right thigh, under your knees. That's right. Now lock his wrists like that, Charlie. Good and tight. We want him secure; we don't give a shit for comfortable, do we?"

Billy was bent over. He twisted his head, staring up at Longarm. "How in hell do you hope to get me over to that train station? I can't walk like this."

"You worry too much, Billy."

"I'll carry you, Billy honey," Fishtail Fanny said.

"Wrong." Longarm shook his head. He handed a second pair of handcuffs to Charlie. "We're just going to say goodbye to you, Miss Fishtail, and leave you over here at the saloon."

"You son of a bitch," she said.

"Sticks and stones, Fanny," Longarm said. "If you'll just pull your skirts up over your thighs. Don't worry about being immodest. If there's a man in here hasn't seen your naked thighs, you can collect five dollars from him after we're gone."

Fishtail Fanny stared at Longarm, venom twisting her soft cheeks and full lips. After a moment she yanked her skirts up about her waist.

"Now lock your arms about your right leg, Fanny. Just like old Billy was kind enough to do."

Fishtail Fanny cursed Longarm back to his fourth generation of ancestors, but she locked her hands under her thighs, which were powdered and as white as a flounder's belly.

His hands trembling, Crazy Charlie quickly locked the handcuffs on her wrists and then leaped back from her. A nervous laugh rippled across the room.

Little Billy Bates watched Longarm unblinkingly, cold and deadly.

"All right, you smartass bastard," Little Billy said. "How do you think to get me across the street to the station and then onto the train?"

"Like this, Billy." Longarm caught the shriveled little man's belt and yanked him upward. Billy dangled, feet and arms off the floor, his head hanging. "You look like cheap luggage. But what the hell."

Watch for

LONGARM IN DEADWOOD

forty-fifth novel in the bold
LONGARM series from Jove

coming in June!

COMING IN AUGUST!

THE BIGGEST, BOLDEST, WILDEST LONGARM EVER!

LONGARM

AND THE LONE STAR LEGEND

Introducing Jessica Starbuck and her sidekick, Kiai...

The Old West Will Never Be the Same Again!!!

DON'T MISS IT!

LONGARM

_____	06515-5	LONGARM #1	$2.25
_____	05899-8	LONGARM AND THE AVENGING ANGELS #3	$1.95
_____	06063-1	LONGARM IN THE INDIAN NATION #5	$1.95
_____	05900-5	LONGARM AND THE LOGGERS #6	$1.95
_____	05901-3	LONGARM AND THE HIGHGRADERS #7	$1.95
_____	05985-4	LONGARM AND THE NESTERS #8	$1.95
_____	05973-0	LONGARM AND THE HATCHET MAN #9	$1.95
_____	06064-X	LONGARM AND THE MOLLY MAGUIRES #10	$1.95
_____	06626-5	LONGARM AND THE TEXAS RANGERS #11	$2.25
_____	05903-X	LONGARM IN LINCOLN COUNTY #12	$1.95
_____	06153-0	LONGARM IN THE SAND HILLS #13	$1.95
_____	06070-4	LONGARM IN LEADVILLE #14	$1.95
_____	05904-8	LONGARM ON THE DEVIL'S TRAIL #151	$1.95
_____	06104-2	LONGARM AND THE MOUNTIES #16	$1.95
_____	06154-9	LONGARM AND THE BANDIT QUEEN #17	$1.95
_____	06155-7	LONGARM ON THE YELLOWSTONE #18	$1.95
_____	05905-6	LONGARM IN THE FOUR COURNERS #19	$1.95

Available at your local bookstore or return this form to:

J **JOVE/BOOK MAILING SERVICE**
P.O. Box 690, Rockville Center, N.Y. 11570

Please enclose 50¢ for postage and handling for one book, 25¢ each add'l book ($1.25 max.). No cash, CODs or stamps. Total amount enclosed: $_____ in check or money order.

NAME_____

ADDRESS_____

CITY_____ STATE/ZIP_____
Allow six weeks for delivery.   SK-5

LONGARM

_____	06627-3 LONGARM AT ROBBER'S ROOST #20	$2.25
_____	06628-1 LONGARM AND THE SHEEPHERDERS #21	$2.25
_____	06156-5 LONGARM AND THE GHOST DANCERS #22	$1.95
_____	05999-4 LONGARM AND THE TOWN TAMER #23	$1.95
_____	06157-3 LONGARM AND THE RAILROADERS #24	$1.95
_____	05974-9 LONGARM ON THE OLD MISSION TRAIL #25	$1.95
_____	06103-4 LONGARM AND THE DRAGON HUNTERS #26	$1.95
_____	06158-1 LONGARM AND THE RURALES #27	$1.95
_____	06629-X LONGARM ON THE HUMBOLDT #28	$2.25
_____	05585-9 LONGARM ON THE BIG MUDDY #29	$1.95
_____	06581-1 LONGARM SOUTH OF THE GILA #30	$2.25
_____	06580-3 LONGARM IN NORTHFIELD #31	$2.25
_____	06582-X LONGARM AND THE GOLDEN LADY #32	$2.25
_____	06583-8 LONGARM AND THE LAREDO LOOP #33	$2.25
_____	06584-6 LONGARM AND THE BOOT HILLERS #34	$2.25
_____	06630-3 LONGARM AND THE BLUE NORTHER #35	$2.25
_____	05591-3 LONGARM ON THE SANTA FE #36	$1.95
_____	05594-8 LONGARM AND THE DEVIL'S RAILROAD #39	$1.95
_____	05596-4 LONGARM IN SILVER CITY #40	$1.95
_____	05597-2 LONGARM ON THE BARBARY COAST #41	$1.95
_____	05598-0 LONGARM AND THE MOONSHINERS #42	$1.95

Available at your local bookstore or return this form to:

J JOVE/BOOK MAILING SERVICE
P.O. Box 690, Rockville Center, N.Y. 11570

Please enclose 75¢ for postage and handling for one book, 25¢
each add'l book ($1.25 max.). No cash, CODs or stamps. Total
amount enclosed: $_____ in check or money order.

NAME_____

ADDRESS_____

CITY_____ _____STATE/ZIP_____

Allow six weeks for delivery.   SK-6